THE SIBYL

By the same author

Mindwire
Mythic

THE SIBYL

Carl Sampson

For Freda and Sonia

PART ONE

DREAMS AND RESISTANCE

1

The information revolution had really begun with the SensApps. Initially, the technology had used the early forms of surveillance developed in the Mindwire program. There had been some concerns over privacy but in the last few years the corporations and the government had undertaken a massive advertising effort to demonstrate the benefits of data-sharing. So it took very little time for the SensApps to take over. People soon forgot the controversy over the fallout of 'Mendesgate' and the government's use of the Mindwire program.

Even though sibyls had increased in numbers and were still employed as data seers by the government and numerous corporations, it was the people, ironically enough, that were spying on themselves through the SensApps. The SensApps were freely downloadable to the devices of the moment, including the new InfoWatch. To the savvy individual, any fragment of information about body or mind processes was available at a glance. The SensApps offered the long held dream of opening up the inner experience of the human mind. Emotional, cognitive and physiological data was heavily number crunched and then fed to the corporations, helping them sell those indispensable products which they considered necessary to life. Life was no longer private, it was part of an immense database — a functional equivalent of life itself stored on huge computers with cloud access.

He stood near the cliff edge. The sky was dark and yet there was a golden light streaming onto the grass and illuminating the rich colours of the small wild flowers. Harebells and speedwells were twitching in a breeze that he could not feel, tiny blue points of light highlighting the gold and green around them.

It began as it always did. He saw her in the distance staring out to sea and he walked slowly towards her. He wanted to talk to her but she couldn't hear him. She didn't even know he was there. No matter how close he moved she still seemed unreachable, as distant as ever. There was still some kind of block. Suddenly the landscape fell, the surroundings fragmenting like pieces of a jigsaw. The connection was lost. It had been like this forever, he thought.

He sat up in bed and lit a cigarette. He watched the grey blue smoke spiral up then gain momentum, carried by a slight draft from the window. He had been having these dreams for the last few years, ever since Amy had disappeared. Recently, he had been contracting a sibyl to form the dreams. As repulsive as it was to him, he had to admit that even dream contact was better than no contact at all.

His job required continual vigilance, leaving him room for little else in his life. You couldn't be sure that someone wasn't looking to stab you in the back in order to give themselves a foothold on the Escherian ladders and stairways that led up to the echelons of power. Deception was central to the game. He had decided that humans were like herd animals, always seeking some kind of nurturing. Give them a little of what they think they want every now and again and you had them like putty in your hands. Let people assume they were safe, secure and well thought of and they would give you everything. It was a psychology of conditioning. In his famous physiology experiments Pavlov had managed to have his dogs drooling at the prospect of whatever food they might receive. This was just as easily applied to humans.

He knew that it was ideas like these that had helped him rise quickly through the ranks. He had never rocked the boat. He was a sound person, reliable, a trustworthy hand. Once you got so far up the organisation your survival was guaranteed. You were no longer in danger of having to get your hands really dirty. There was always someone lower down the chain desperate to progress who would do your dirty work for you. For it was only the elite that possessed any real freedom. After all, they were the masters of the game.

Carla sat up and looked at the clock. It was 2:00 a.m. She had no other appointments booked in for tonight. She turned the table lamp on and reached for some water. She switched the InfoWatch to non-broadcast mode and sipped the water, swirling the last few inches of water around in the glass. The beginning of a dream was like listening to water dripping, dribbling, coursing steadily with a direction of its own. The trick was to hold on to the pattern. It was like watching a ripple but not following it away downstream, holding on instead to the pattern underneath that creates the ripple. When the dream was in full flow it felt more like a land-locked lake, still but pulsating slowly, almost too slow to be noticeable. But with practice she had become sensitive to slight changes in the pulse and she had realised it was the best way of figuring out where you were with the dream.

This dream had slipped into existence smoothly, as it always did, but it barely ever developed to a slow, regular flowing pulse. These subtleties were unique signatures, as individual as finger prints or the crystalline patterns of the human iris. He was regular, this client. He had been dreaming through her for the last two months and had paid up front for four months. She had never met him but he kept coming back; his sessions had increased to three times a week now from the typical once a fortnight. He clearly wanted this dream but could not move beyond a certain stage.

She lay back on the bed, cradling her head with her hands, fingers interlaced. She deepened her breathing and slipped into another dream, one of her own this time. Water slowly enveloped her toes and ankles and soon she was fully immersed. The water was warm and the ripples glistened in the sunlight. She was looking out to sea. She kicked her legs and pushed against the water, turning to see land. The beach was pure white and seemed to stretch out for miles, empty and silent. This tropical paradise was her way of cleaning herself. She knew that it was a clichéd image, but it helped her wash away her contact with the clients and feel herself clean of their emotions and concerns.

2

Louie stepped off the train and checked his InfoWatch. The time was 8:00 a.m. More importantly, his watch was showing ninety per cent maximal functioning. Data upload was normal, although he had lost a few minutes of real time upload during the journey through the tunnel. There were only a few discrepancies in terms of ideal self-composition.

He almost couldn't remember a time when he wasn't recording his sense status full time. The real time upload analysis meant that he could record his status anywhere and get a report whenever he wanted one. Of course, it offered certain benefits: he had been paid thirty pounds last month just for his ten physiological data streams. As well as the money, he received a full spectrum health report every week. It was surprising that sometimes he felt quite good but the reports indicated that his physiological functioning was below par. But he trusted the analysis: there must be something wrong.

It was 8:20 a.m. and he was on his way to school. At twenty-four he looked young, but he had grown a full — if somewhat scraggly — beard to make himself look older. Some parents commented on how young the teachers looked these days and he always thought that the comments were aimed at him, although he was the sixth oldest teacher in the school. He thought the beard gave him gravitas.

He had woken on time this morning. He had an app which helped him sleep properly; he could set it to wake him when he was in a light sleep at a time approximate to the time he needed to get up. He took the shortest route to school, but power-walked. The movement sensor in his watch recorded the number and pace of the steps and calculated the distance he had travelled. Uploading was automatic after he had stopped moving and he could review his results on a tablet or his phone; they offered a bit more screen real estate for viewing than his InfoWatch.

At the school gates there was the usual chaos of parents dropping off their children. He barely noticed a young blond woman standing alone by the gate as he rushed past. One blink and she was gone.

He grabbed a coffee in the staff room. He could see other teachers surveying their data streams. One by one, personal alarms went off to indicate it was their time to go and teach. Only McAndrews was temporarily offline. He had been reprimanded three times this year for wrapping his watch in aluminium foil, effectively insulating the device from the readers in the locality and disturbing real-time upload. McAndrews stared into space, lost in his own thoughts. He seemed to have found an oasis of calm in a sea of digitised havoc.

Louie began his class. He held his watch up and the camera took the register, the face recognition program automatically engaging and recording who was present. It was a very short process since there were only three students in class today. Most would be taking their lessons remotely and were at home or somewhere else. Rachel and Tommy were checking their watches and streaming the lesson to their tablets. They wore headphones with microphones attached and swiped and tapped the glass surface of the tablet to indicate which of the multiple choice answers in front of them were correct.

Charlotte sat alone. Without her watch, she was having to connect her tablet directly to the class stream. She had dropped her watch again. She was clumsy and seemed to drop it all too often. If she was honest with herself, she didn't like the watch so she gave it less care than it deserved. At six years old she had decided that it messed up her thinking. She had a similar dislike of her computer at home; instead, she spent more time with books. She liked the feel and smell of the paper. Her father had lots of books. She had tried counting them; she had managed a shelf but each time she had come to a different total. He had twenty shelves, she was sure that was a lot of books. They were hard to get today; something about the paper, it was expensive and damaged the earth. She wasn't sure how a book could damage the earth, making 'car bun doxhide', or something like that.

Charlotte did not like school much at all. She particularly dreaded the tests they had every week. Each pupil's test scores were recorded and displayed on the large screen in their classroom for everyone to see all the time. Each student was represented by a picture of themselves which grew taller as their test results improved. She was little in real life and she hated that her picture was the shortest of them all because she was not doing so well in school.

She preferred being at home. Most of her friends seemed to spend lots of time playing games with each other on the net, but she liked to talk with her mum and dad. Her dad was a psychologist, so he talked and listened for a living and was good at it. She knew that her mum worked with the 'mental people' too, and so was used to listening a lot.

'Charlotte, you have selected the wrong lesson.' Louie's watch had chimed in with a student speed and consistency warning. He took remote control of her tablet and set her working on the right lesson. As Charlotte had now started five minutes late, the lesson regulator program flashed up an amber warning on her tablet indicating that she would have to speed up in order to finish the lesson as scheduled. She knew that she could lose points, and more importantly, her image on the big screen in the class would shrink a little again. She rushed to complete the multiple-choice questions.

After the class was dismissed, Louie gave Charlotte a note for her to give to her parents. As she was behind again on aggregate scores, the class-monitoring program had automatically printed up some suggestions to improve her performance. As she left the room clutching the note she noticed that her picture on the large screen overlooking the room had shrunk slightly; she was definitely the shortest now. Gloomily, she walked out to get lunch.

Charlotte always ate her lunch with her friends Ellie and Jane. They were in the year below her but the three of them were often taken for sisters. Charlotte opened her lunch box and nibbled a little of her salad and sandwich. She looked at the time on Ellie's watch and sighed. Hours to go yet. Chewing on her sandwich she began to drift off into daydreams. She was good at dreaming. Her mother had told her that she was clever and dreamy at the same time, which she liked. She took another bite of sandwich: tuna and sweetcorn. She liked sweetcorn; she liked the sweet taste but she especially liked the way it popped when you bit it. She imagined a corn on the cob character dancing in front of her, reaching out and feigning taking her sandwich off her. He was simultaneously rubbing his tummy with circular patterns and smacking his lips in anticipation of having some of her sandwich. She giggled at the figure. Ellie and Jane tuned in and laughed at the image Charlotte had created. The image changed as Ellie imagined the cobman standing under a large pot of cream and soon to be drenched and dripping. Charlotte laughed, and Jane giggled and dropped her sandwich.

3

Marsden was checking the materials for his talk. He went through the document, editing expertly, practised at the task. He had been a university lecturer, specialising in anthropology, until a year ago when he had opted for voluntary redundancy. He had felt more and more out of step with modern academia. He would be the first to admit that he was 'old world'. At sixty-two, he felt more like six hundred these days. The modern world was one of plastic, logic, a science that assumed the naive simplicity of Occam's razor. He hated this poverty-stricken view. He himself, on the other hand, saw the world as complex, multileveled and organic. As a boy growing up in Africa, he had spent most nights sleeping out in the bush; he traded salt with natives, learnt to track animals. His teenage years had not been spent playing with computer games — they barely existed then — or racing around like young lads today on motorbikes that sounded like hair dryers, or even flirting with girls. Instead, he had become friendly with the local wise man, a 'witch doctor'. The wise man was an expert in understanding the way that people constructed their worlds. Custom, culture and ultimately imagination were the building blocks. He was not a classic magician, but he understood the unconscious human processes within which people operated. He was sure-footed when it came to assessing the cadence, complexity and constantly shifting balance of the human interaction process.

It saddened Marsden that today most people were losing this ability. Minds, he thought, were like dances, constantly revolving around an axis but shifting all the time, making allowances, signalling directions, only to return to the centre time and time again. Nowadays that dance was being limited by the constraints of the digital world. Organic amorphous minds were being forced into perfect geometry. It didn't work; it meant lopping off any aspects that didn't fit.

As an anthropologist, he had spent a good deal of time away from Britain: China, Papua New Guinea and of course his beloved Africa. He had spent part of the last few years in Africa studying death rituals. Death was the point at which people were really up against life; the sharp contrast created a tension which had to be safely defused. The rituals he had studied were a dance between what was known and what was unknown, easing and smoothing the edges of the two territories. The bushmen he had lived with in Africa still had a sense of the balance between these two domains, although even their view of the world was changing fast. Nearly everyone, even in the most isolated communities, now had InfoWatches; it was revolutionising life in Africa, but in his last few visits he had witnessed the cost.

'Dr Marsden, are you ready? I think everyone is in and seated now.'

Thomas Jones, the organiser of the talks for the Neoluddites society, was leaning across the table to address him. Jones looked quickly at his pocket watch and checked the time. Marsden watched Jones's movements, the way he grasped his watch from its pocket, loosening the chain and flipping open the cover to reveal a beautiful nineteenth century case. It was funny that even machine haters like the Luddites still accepted mechanical watches, but there was something about a clockwork watch that made it feel alive and organic.

'Yes, all ready, do you want to introduce me now?'

'Yes, I will. You have forty minutes for the talk and fifteen minutes or so for questions, is that alright?'

'Fine, no problem.'

Jones moved forward on the stage slowly and gestured to draw people's attention to the next talk on the programme.

'Ladies and Gentleman, we are very pleased to have Dr Alan Marsden here tonight to give us a talk on the past and the present. As you probably know, he was an academic who has spent a good a good deal of his life studying what makes us human. He published the classic text, Human Behaviour: Primitive and Modern . . .'

Marsden stopped listening to Jones and looked into the crowd. There was the usual mix of young and old, male and female, but his eye was caught by some unexpected attendees sitting near the back. Their presence was signalled by a constant twitching and raising of arms as they checked their InfoWatches. They were clearly mechanophiles even though they had played down the technology to get in tonight. That spelled trouble, he thought.

'Ladies and Gentleman, I give you Dr Alan Marsden.'

'Thank you, Mr Jones, for your generous introduction; I hope I won't let you down.'

Marsden smiled broadly at Jones, who was already hand in pocket looking for his watch as he searched for his seat.

'I would like to begin, Ladies and Gentlemen, by giving you a little indication of how the human mind has changed. It will be a broad brushstroke account, going back centuries and even millennia. However, I believe we are at a juncture where something interesting is going to happen.'

In the back row, Louie fidgeted in his chair. He was sitting with his friends, Ron and Mandy. It was another night out sop-baiting. The three of them had been to a talk on the paranormal last week and had baited the speaker until she had almost cried. It was important, Louie thought, that these charlatans were outed for their woolly thoughts and religious inclinations.

He was barely listening to Marsden because his InfoWatch had indicated a sudden drop in physiological functioning. The watch's display suggested that it correlated significantly with eating the speciality burger at the Happy House cafe just before they had come to the talk. Louie started worrying that he might have food poisoning. Sodding bacteria. He sometimes wished that sanitised foods like the complete supplements he had read about in his *Science Now* magazine were further along in development than they currently were. That would mean that he could avoid eating real food with all its inherent dangers.

Mandy was nearly there, he thought. She swore that 'Carbs were the enemy'. So she avoided all starchy foods and since she was unsure about eating fruit and vegetables, especially the fresh kind, she had limited herself to meat, the kind that was a long way down the processing line and could not be identified as deriving from any particular part of any particular animal. He glanced over at Mandy and saw that she was checking her calorie consumption for the day on her InfoWatch.

'In thinking about the development of the modern mind,' Marsden was saying, 'One thing I have to address is the ubiquitous use of computing devices and the current obsession with big data.' He was getting into his stride.

Louie started paying attention. Here it comes, he thought. It was always an attack on the modern by these dinosaurs. He felt sometimes as if he was an apostle of the machine.

'There is a cumulative effect from using these devices. Problems with attention have been noticed, especially in young children. Not to mention the health problems that might derive from overuse of devices with high frequency radio output. I think the most troubling issue for the human mind is the assumption that the mind and its thoughts can be treated as data. These are the questions we must ask: Who has access to our personal data? How is it being used? What is it being used for?' Marsden paused and looked at the audience. The back row looked like it was about to erupt.

'Can I ask a question?' Louie was holding his arm aloft and standing up to maximise his presence.

'Questions are usually saved for the end of the talk . . .' Jones, the chairman, half-stood to address Louie and then sank back to his seat.

'It is important to ask it now,' Louie insisted, 'before Dr Marsden gets carried away with a prejudiced diatribe on the modern world.'

Jones started to stand again.

'I am happy to answer the young man's question.' Marsden gestured to Jones.

Louie was warming to his topic. 'I would just like to ensure that Dr Marsden recognises the great progress that science and technology have made in the twenty-first century. For instance, our medical knowledge has never been better and people are living much longer than ever. This is due to a better understanding of our world and the dramatic surge in technological development.'

'I think that there are always benefits and hazards involved in human behaviour,' Marsden said. 'The main problem is that even in science it is hard to rule out self-interest and politics, and that is where the worst hazards lie.'

'You haven't responded to my examples of improved health and people living longer,' Louie retorted. He was sure he had Marsden on the run.

'Well, it is true that medical techniques and assessment have become ever more elaborate, but do you know what is the biggest killer? The doctors themselves. More people die because of medical interventions, so-called iatrogenic cases, than from any other single cause. In terms of people living longer, it depends where you look and how you do the calculations. Individuals in some cultures have regularly lived past a hundred. One problem with the calculations is that there was high infant mortality in the past, so any estimates of the average age of death are always low. Generally, however, if people survived childhood they lived well into their nineties, especially outside of the cities. So things are not as clear-cut as you might think.'

'I think they are; you just have to avoid fuzzy thinking and keep up the important data gathering that is a fundamental part of modern life. It's central to having more control over life.' Louie was becoming a little hot under the collar.

'That is only your opinion, of course. Opinions are the basis of thought, but they are not facts,' said Marsden.

'I'm only interested in facts!' Louie shouted.

Jones had been attempting to take control of the discussion but

21

the exchange had been too rapid. He now stood and suggested that Marsden continue with his talk and that any other questions be saved for the end.

Marsden resumed, making a series of points about the mind not being suitable for digitisation. Louie was fuming. He hated losing his cool. Perhaps it was his stomach problem. To his annoyance, Marsden seemed barely ruffled. Louie and his friends shifted uncomfortably in the back row, now bored with the talk and Marsden's obvious stuck-in-the-mud attitude. They amused themselves by repeatedly checking their wrists for any new data arriving.

4

Paul glanced at the TV screen as he put down his book. The TV was rarely on these days. There was nothing worth watching, but Sadie had put the evening news on. The Day Centre had had a visit from a politician today and so she was keen to catch the story on the local news.

'Here it comes.' Sadie was clapping her hands excitedly and smiling at Charlotte. Charlotte joined in even though she wasn't sure what it was for.

The news story showed the minister for mental health walking around the Centre talking briefly to various clients. She had managed to maintain a sympathetic expression until Freddie had accidentally dropped the flowers that were a gift from the centre when he went to shake her hand. Her smile had faded at this point and she had insisted that the cameraman do a second take. Next, she was shown shaking hands with Sadie.

'I knew I shouldn't have opted for that dress, it makes my bottom look huge.' She looked over at Paul but he was engrossed in his book.

'You should have worn your green dress, Mummy,' Charlotte said.

Sadie turned to Charlotte and hugged her while trying to nibble her ears. Charlotte giggled and struggled to get free.

On the TV screen, the minister's visit was over and she left amidst promises for support. A commercial break started with an advert for a clothing company featuring an actress in a bright green dress smoothing the material across her hips. The music that accompanied the advert was one of Sadie's favourite songs and she started humming along absent-mindedly. Charlotte pointed at the screen.

'Get this dress, Mummy!'

A weather broadcast began on the TV. The meteorological content was short and sweet — some sun to be followed by showers. The forecaster then switched to an enthusiastic account of the economic climate.

'The current high consumption front is likely to move in from the west for the next three days before cooling down to moderate purchases next weekend. There may be some decline in consumption for the next week or two before a resurgence in the medium term. It is expected that the forecasted skirmishes in the Middle East will generate some decline in the commodities markets prior to the elections, and create a price rise in oil derivatives in the near future.' The forecaster looked pleased with his account and then wished viewers a good shopping weekend. Paul turned the TV off, groaning at the obsession with prediction based on spurious data.

'Don't say it!' Sadie smiled at him.

He smiled back and didn't say anything. He felt more and more that their house was a bunker against a maddening world. Things had changed so fast. Since Charlotte Mendes had died, he couldn't believe how the pace of life had speeded up. He could see now that what had happened with Charlotte had been a forerunner of things to come. The paradigm of technological control that she had lashed back at had exploded overnight. It was like one of those flowers with seed heads that under the right conditions just burst violently, haemorrhaging seeds everywhere. The technology that had once seemed so outlandish was now built into everyone's personal devices. Watches had completely replaced mobile phones. They responded to voice instructions; no need for clumsy finger tapping, although most people used this in public places because of background noise. They also had the same sensor technology that had been developed for the sibyl seers. This software detected changes in physiology and emotion. Once a user had ticked the box agreeing to the contract for the software, they had signed away their rights to any privacy. Personal information was constantly uploaded to the cloud, ready for various corporations to feed off.

In Paul's opinion, the SensApps almost made thinking unnecessary and nearly impossible if you tried. The SensApps were a constant presence, recording, beeping alerts, needing responses and demanding interaction. He hated them and the idea behind them. It seemed like Charlotte's death had been a license for the governments and corporations to do openly what they had been doing covertly for years. But almost everyone had upgraded to the InfoWatch, social networks and life applications all included. The watches were even being accepted as valid forms of identification instead of passports and driving licenses. No one seemed to mind that their privacy had been heisted completely. Somewhere on a computer database everyone's physiological, emotional, consumption and location data was being recorded every millisecond of the day.

Of course, he knew that it was all a matter of freedom of choice; no one was forced to wear the watches, but it was clear nearly everyone did. And of course there were incentives: digital brownies could be collected and used in return for cash or purchases. A whole new Internet had been developed purely for the traffic of personal data collected by the info devices. The whole concept had been an outgrowth of projects in the United States to create a permanent database family for all emails and digital transactions. A shadow of the World Wide Web, it was named the ConnectWeb, a name which some people had started to shorten to ConWeb without necessarily picking up on the alternative meaning.

The authorities had made it known that they no longer needed sibyls; the watches and ConWeb meant that everyone was now directly monitored. Increasingly, the sibyls were seen as possible terrorists and Paul was sure that they would soon be required to wear the watches all the time. As a consequence, sibyls were often considered outcasts or scapegoats. Paul himself was not convinced that the governments had given up on using them. Rumours constantly circulated that sibyls were still employed filtering and sorting the data that was gathered from all sources, including CCTV. Paul had read that the UK now had more surveillance cameras per person than the People's Republic of China. But the growing paranoia about surveillance was often focused on the sibyls rather than on governments. They had become an underclass overnight. Charlotte Mendes had embarrassed the security services and governments and across the Western world the reverberations were felt high up the political and corporate chain of command. Politicians had decried the actions of some mavericks, and insisted that once the new transparency information bill was enacted, covert operations like Project Mindwire would be impossible.

But the numbers of sibyls had continued to increase and no one seemed to have any explanation for this. Now there were girls with the likeness of Charlotte on every street corner. Scientists had no explanations for the sudden surge in sibyl numbers. The politicians used them as scapegoats and the general public were distrustful — until one appeared in their family of course. They were almost seen as aliens and Paul could imagine that if they hadn't had family ties they would have probably been put in concentration camps. Instead, they were relegated to scraping a living as fortune tellers, offering psychic nuggets for a few coins. Some sibyls took advantage of the new InfoWatch technology, tapping into it to create dreams for others.

Paul sometimes found himself watching the sibyls when he was around town. It was odd, he thought, that when you did see a few sibyls together they exchanged hugs but hardly said anything. Their watches monitored their location and their association in numbers was not encouraged since the Charlotte Mendes affair. It had quickly been forgotten that the Mindwire project had psychiatrically imprisoned more than a hundred young women. Some had recovered and left the hospitals, but some were too damaged and had to stay. Suicide had been all too common among those sibyls.

Paul still found it difficult to think that Charlotte was really dead, especially with doppelgängers at what seemed like every turn. And when he looked at his own daughter, who they had named in memory of Charlotte, he thought he could see a sibyl in development. She was small, which was surprising because Sadie and he were above average height. She was intuitive and found it very difficult to deal with the academic rigours of school. She hated maths but could often come up with the right answer anyway with no calculations involved. He and Sadie had once or twice discussed the possibility of Charlotte being a sibyl but otherwise avoided thinking too much about the possibility.

Louie waited for his drinks machine to produce a coffee. He was annoyed that he hadn't been able to rile Marsden enough to torpedo his talk. That kind of claptrap was an affront to any thinking man's philosophy. It was obvious that the modern world was far better than the past and that the development of machines and technology had been the main contributor to this improvement. Folks like Marsden were just stuck in the mud. He was still waiting impatiently for his coffee when the machine sent an error message to his watch. Annoyed, he made a note of the error message — ERROR 135B. He would have to return the machine to the rental firm for maintenance tomorrow. He took some CoolCaff from the fridge and swigged from the bottle.

He had been a member of the Technophile Society for two years now and had been to every meeting and conference. He had thought it important to take an active role in the society, and as far as he was concerned that involved baiting as many of the Neoluddites as he could. They were just simpletons; they couldn't see what was right in front of them. They were sceptical about the new technological developments but failed to see the benefits. Louie blamed a lot of this on the stupid projects involving the dullard girls, the so-called sibyls. For instance, the banks had tried to use them to intuitively bet on the markets, but inevitably it had been a failure. A large-scale economic crisis had been the result and the governments had had to bail out the banks. Now everyone was paying for the sibyls' failures. Some said that the banks' own betting on the markets had caused the problem and that the sibyls were just patsies. But in Louie's opinion, the sibyls had to be the root of the problem; a lack of rational thinking could only lead to disaster.

Carla's mother had phoned to set up the appointment so Paul had not even spoken to Carla, but her soft voice stirred his memories. She sounded so much like Charlotte Mendes. Rising slowly and calmly from the chair in the waiting room she stepped into the office. She turned towards Paul as she dropped her dark coloured hood and he was able to see her face properly for the first time. He was astonished; not only did she sound like Charlotte, she also looked like her. There were small differences of course, but these were mostly outweighed by similarities. She was small and fine-boned with the darkest of eyes. Even the way she watched Paul as he began to speak reminded him of Charlotte: the posture, the little nods of agreement that pepper any conversation in order to maintain the bond and the flow. There was something else too. He had the feeling he had met her before, but knew that was impossible.

'What can I do for you, Carla?'

'Where to begin?' Her eyes flickered to and fro, looking around the room.

'Just relax, take your time. We're not in a rush,' Paul reassured her.

'Unfortunately, I think I am Dr Clark.'

'Call me Paul. What do you mean?'

'Well, you have obviously noted my appearance. We have officially been labelled "liminals" but the term "sibyl" may have more meaning for you.' She suddenly looked defensive. Her hands were clasped but her fingers were constantly active, nervous.

'Yes, I am familiar with the terms . . . I think it is unnecessary. I don't agree with the authorities labelling you this way.' Paul felt uncomfortable, as if he was in some way responsible.

'The labelling does make things difficult, for others more than me. At least I make a living,' she said. 'Anyway, my problem is

28

that . . . well, it's my dreaming.'

She made first contact with Paul's gaze. Her eyes shone like black polished stones. She hesitated, then obviously reached some kind of decision.

'My dreaming is becoming real.' She seemed relieved to have got the words out.

Paul was concerned. Being unable to discern reality from dreams — so-called 'reality monitoring' — often led to psychosis. He had heard of more and more sibyls becoming hospitalised because of their inability to distinguish between fantasy and reality.

'Could you give me an example?'

Carla's head hung low. She now raised it to meet Paul's gaze again.

'I have been dreaming things into being.'

'What do you mean by "into being?"'

'My dreams are starting to take place in reality.'

'Do you mean that your dreams are anticipating events that happen, like precognition — have you heard of that?'

'Sensing things in advance of them happening, yes, I know what that means. This is more complicated. I can make choices in dreams . . . did you know that the sibyls can do this?'

'No. Tell me about it.' If he was understanding Carla properly, this was a whole new ball game.

'Some people can control their dreams . . . it requires a sense of partly being awake while dreaming. I have heard it called lucid dreaming, are you familiar with that?'

Paul nodded. 'Yes, I know about lucid dreaming, go on.'

'Well, sibyls can dream lucidly, but what has started to happen in my dreams — and it's happening to some of my friends too — is that we can make choices in our dreams, but then we encounter situations in waking life which correspond to the dream. The dream depicts the situation in advance, like precognition, but then the choices appear too. In some way, our dreams are influencing reality.'

She sighed, as if this was a kind of unburdening.

'Could it be that you feel you are making choices but in fact some level of the unconscious mind, the author of the dream, is still actually involved?'

Paul was sceptical that the sibyls could do what Carla said. More worryingly, this could be a confusion signifying psychological problems.

She shook her head.

'It started with small things.' She hesitated. 'It sounds silly, but I had a dream with my friend in it where she changed her hair — or rather I made a choice for her and changed it totally to a bright blond colour! The next time I saw her, her hair was as I had seen it in the dream.'

'Had you talked with her about changing her hair? It could have been a coincidence.'

'No, we had never spoken about her hair and this happened the day immediately after I had dreamt it. But this is just a small and trivial example of what I am experiencing now almost every day.'

As Carla left after their hour-long session Paul had the curious thought that this was familiar. Curiously, he had dreamt recently of spending time with a group of sibyls learning to create dreams. Was *he* seeing things in dreams now?

5

Reading the newspaper over breakfast, Marsden's attention was caught by a story about a fight between three women outside the local supermarket. Unusual, he thought, that the protagonists were women but even more so that one of them was a sibyl. Apparently, one of the women had accused the sibyl of sleeping with her husband. The sibyl denied the accusation but still left the scene bleeding. She was picked up by the emergency services and the police because her InfoWatch had transmitted an emergency physiological status message to the Department of Intelligence Analysis, or DIA.

'It's hard to believe what things are coming to.' Marsden's wife Jenny was peering over his shoulder at the newspaper.

'This fight story you mean?' He turned to face Jenny. 'Yes, it is surprising,' he agreed.

Jenny disappeared into the kitchen and returned a couple of minutes later with a pot of tea.

'The sibyl girl argued that it was a dream. She said that she had never seen the woman before and that she had never met her husband, never mind slept with him. Odd isn't it?'

'Odd?' Marsden asked.

'Yes, it's a little strange. Nancy told me about three or four other instances that have happened recently.'

'What, fights between women?'

'Fights between women where a sibyl is involved and is accused of various things. Sometimes it's over men, sometimes over clothes, also over—'

'Clothes?'

'Nancy was in the dry cleaners and a sibyl came in to collect some clothes. The shop assistant set about her, saying that the sibyl had destroyed some clothes she had been working on. What's surprising is that the sibyl denied it calmly, but she didn't seem surprised at all. She just turned and walked out. Presumably she got someone else to pick up her clothes . . .' Jenny tapered off and gazed at the table. 'Do you think this tablecloth needs changing?'

Marsden was wrapped up in his own thoughts and didn't answer. The sibyls were finding trouble wherever they went; no wonder they couldn't find jobs. He had met a few who had been students when he was teaching and they had struck him as amiable and conscientious. He couldn't believe the rapidity with which these people had become an underclass. It wasn't based on race, since sibyls included all ethnic types. Most sibyls were females, but there were males appearing now with some of the same intuitive characteristics of the female sibyls. He was not sure he liked the official term 'liminals'; it automatically put them outside normal society. He was completely against the enforced monitoring they had to undergo. It had been more than five years now since the Charlotte Mendes event that had led to the monitoring in the first place. He had heard that a number of psychiatric hospitals had been complicit in holding individuals who had been involved in the Mindwire project. Pouring himself more tea, Marsden returned to his paper.

Charlotte snuggled up to her teddy. She was wearing her favourite pyjamas, which also featured a slightly psychedelic teddy bear pattern. She fell into a restless sleep populated by scattered images and strained dreams.

She was in a shop. Mummy had been there next to her holding her hand, but now she had gone and Charlotte couldn't see her anywhere. She looked around but there was no one in the shop except for her. Then, out of the corner of her eye she saw a lady who was standing very still. Only her eyes moved as she looked at Charlotte. Then three older girls came into the shop and started shouting at the lady, throwing things at her and hitting her. The lady didn't move or shout; she didn't respond at all. Then Daddy appeared and took her out of the shop and gave her her teddy to carry.

6

Louie looked through the ten pages of the lesson he had prepared. He was pleased with it. He had used TeachMap, a free application that operated on all types of devices. It was free because it relied on advertising for revenue generation, but since all schools now embedded advertising in lessons anyway it made sense to use the app for lesson construction. The children used it at home to do their homework and the program ensured that every twelve minutes they would have a little commercial break.

They were doing biology today. Charlotte hated it. She couldn't remember the names of the bits of the body. Why anybody would want to mystified her.

Louie's lesson began with a quiz to test their knowledge of the topics covered in the last lesson. Each of the children looked at their tablet computers as a range of shapes appeared on the screen. Bones and organs spun into existence one at a time, with some multiple-choice options at the side. Touch the right answer, the program gave you a point; get it wrong and a point was subtracted from your final score. To make it more fun, Louie had built in comedy noises which audibly indicated success or failure for each choice.

They started the test and there was a cacophony of successful and unsuccessful sounds. The successful sounds consisted of balloons bursting, champagne corks popping. The negative ones were raspberry sounds, mouth-formed farts, which made the children laugh.

As a picture of a heart appeared and rotated on her tablet, Charlotte was slow to decide. The heart flashed, as if impatient for an answer. She tapped the multiple-choice answer for heart. Pop! Next it was a bone, a tibia she thought. Pop! The next question was harder. It asked for the location of the liver. She didn't like the taste of liver so she decided that it should be reasonably distant from her mouth. She tapped the diagram of the body near the belly. Fart! Wrong answer. *Who cares?* she thought. She couldn't imagine when she would ever need to know where a liver was.

Louie monitored the scoring in real time and projected the results to a common screen in the class, showing each child's score as their guesses increased or decreased their point total. Charlotte lingered near the bottom of the class as usual. He considered printing another note for her parents but decided to hold back. He would see them later that week at the parents' evening. He quickly took the results of her tests so far that year, calculated averages and measures of variability, and put them on a digital note to refer back to later.

After his last class, Louie caught the Tube home. He felt a little under the weather. The forecasted arrival time on his watch was out by thirty seconds. Something had to be wrong somewhere as he had checked his watch earlier that morning, calibrating it with the standard local time estimates. He thought it was ironic that the more a person became concerned about the exactness of the world, the more they were dissatisfied with inexact measurements. He checked his watch again to see what the time was. Staring at the digital readout, he watched the seconds, small parcels of time spinning away. The more he stared, the more the intervals seemed to extend until each second seemed elastic.

He was sitting near the Tube train entrance doors and he watched them open and close. They seemed slower than normal. He listened for the beat of his heart, but he couldn't hear or feel it. Checking his watch, he brought up his physiology readings. His pulse was 72 bpm, blood pressure 140/90; the blood pressure was flashing amber. Respiration was at 60% efficiency and dropping. He looked around nervously; he was starting to feel nauseous. His watch started to pulse against his skin, it was in silent mode and was requesting that he should read and respond to some of its messages.

A blond girl across the carriage was quietly watching as Louie was tapping and swiping his watch face furiously. Focused only on the watch, Louie managed to miss his stop because he had to open his rucksack to stop his tablet and phone from chirruping the same requests to respond to his unusual physiological status measures. He knew that if he left it too long, the watch would contact the train's sensors and everyone would assume he was an emergency case.

After having walked back a station in the rain, he reached home, peeled off his wet clothes and fell into bed. His forehead was hot and he had started sneezing. His thoughts returned to how he had felt on the train. It came to him that there was an obvious explanation. They called it 'data confusion syndrome'. Occasional data overload could at times cause confused states of awareness, especially in the early adopters of new technology with broad data catchment. Feedback loops between the brain and data-gathering devices like the InfoWatches were set up to act like audio feedback, creating temporary data–reality misalignment.

He sighed with relief; he had satisfactorily explained his response on the train. There was a rational explanation for everything. He sneezed. He felt his hot forehead again then dropped into a confused sleep as his watch quietly chirruped itself to silence.

Opening the door of his office, Paul saw Carla already waiting. They exchanged a few pleasantries and she sat on the couch.

'I've had more of those dreams. Most of my dreams now are predicting day-to-day reality. What's more disturbing is that there are commonalities between the dreams. I'm dreaming the same dreams as my friends.'

'What are the dreams about?'

'The most recurrent one is about the sibyls. In the dreams, they're acting like zombies. They have no volition of their own but there is something controlling them. This goes beyond mandatory use of the InfoWatch; it's something more fundamental which allows complete control. And I keep touching the back of my neck as if there's something there.'

'You say that other sibyls are having the same dreams?'

She nodded and sighed. 'What's happening, Paul?'

7

'It's staring at me, Mummy.'

'What do you mean, Charlotte?'

'It's staring at me,' Charlotte insisted.

Sadie looked at the mannequin, her gaze eventually settling on the eyes; they were quite realistic for a shop dummy. She held her hand to her eyes to shield them from the sunlight coming through the large plate glass window. The eyes were extraordinarily lifelike, and as she stared she thought she saw something move, some subtle internal adjustment.

'Can I ask you what you're doing, madam?'

An officious voice interrupted her thoughts. A female security guard had quietly approached and was standing behind Sadie. Charlotte was hiding behind Sadie's legs.

'I thought I saw its eyes move . . . I was just curious.'

'Oh, that's fine.' The security guard was obviously relieved. 'These are our new models, the cloneXB1; they have cameras in the eyes and face-recognition programming. They can tell if you like the clothes they're displaying.'

The guard smiled, as if amazed at the ingenuity of the technology. Sadie stared at her in disbelief. The guard continued to explain.

'I was worried that you might break it. We had some young sibyls in here the other day and they made a scene about the model and jammed a screwdriver into its eye sockets.'

Charlotte was now squeezing Sadie's right leg tightly. Sadie picked her up and walked to the exit, glancing uneasily at the other mannequins along the path to the doors.

'It was staring at me, Mummy.'

'I know, chicken, I know it was. We'll go home now.'

The Ayers Arms was the pub of choice for the rationalist groups. Louie returned to his seat behind the table and picked up his drink. His glass was nearly empty. He would have to venture to the bar again, but at this time of day the crowd waiting was at least three people deep.

Mandy was looking at her watch and tapping the glass screen.

'Twelve hundred calories today . . . I don't believe it! Where did they come from? Talk about hidden calories.' She looked briefly at Louie but saw that he was staring into space. She checked her watch again, searching through the day's record of what she had eaten.

Louie was watching a sibyl moving in front of the bar. She didn't look like most of the other sibyls but he was convinced she had to be one. They were just fakes. It was as simple as that. Personally, he didn't think they needed monitoring or shunning in society, they just needed re-educating. It was impossible to do what they believed they could do. Louie didn't believe in extrasensory perception, it was not possible, not plausible even. Evolution had brought humans to the current peak of development and technology had taken them further. It was just superstition, poor critical thinking, just 'woo'!

Just as his ire was peaking, the sibyl walked over to their table carrying some glasses on a tray. She put a glass of lager down on the table and a tonic water in front of Mandy.

'Sibyls as barmaids now?' sneered Mandy.

'That'll be four pounds fifty please.' The sibyl looked implacable.

'Why?' stammered Louie.

'Because it's three pounds for the beer and one pound fifty for the water,' she said patiently.

'No, I mean why did you bring us these?'

'Intuition, sir. We operate an intuitive service during happy hour to keep the numbers down at the bar.'

She smiled, picked up the little pile of coins Louie had stacked on the tray and walked back to the bar.

'Flim flam,' said Mandy and turned back to her phone to run another calories check.

'Even here,' fumed Louie.

They had held their meetings here for five years but the message hadn't seemed to get across to the pub owners.

'You okay, Lou?'

Ron was tall, six foot five, and he wore a long leather trench coat which made him seem even taller.

Louie grasped the hand that Ron offered and gave it a firm shake.

'Yes, fine. Do you know there's a sibyl serving here now?'

'Yeah, pitiful isn't it?'

'It shouldn't be allowed.'

'Right. How's the planning going?'

'Well, we've been waiting for you, genius.'

'Oh yeah, right.'

Ron sat down and tried to gather his coat behind him but it knocked the table and the glasses wobbled.

'Mand, pull up another seat for Ron's coat.'

'Leave it out, Louie. It's got classic style and it's on trend.'

'Just a shame there's so much of it. Mandy! I didn't mean it literally.'

'Do this, do that, what did your last one die of?' She pushed the chair she'd dragged over back to the adjacent table and took the opportunity to see how many calories she had burned off in the act.

'How's the diet going, Mand?' asked Ron, trying to smooth the waters.

'Don't ask!' She brushed her hair back and scowled. 'I'm wondering if it's water retention . . .'

Ron shrugged at Louie and smiled.

Paul and Sadie parked the car in the school car park and followed the signs directing people to the parents' evening. Paul hated these events. It seemed to him that the teachers were getting younger and younger. They had that youthful optimism which lacked the temper of a healthy scepticism about society. Older teachers, who were more questioning, seemed to be in short supply. Life experience wasn't needed when you had all the gadgetry to help teach. The technology was expensive but it was subsidised, making it more appealing to head teachers than an expensive payroll. He knew that teachers on short-term contracts tended to do what they were told. Paul couldn't help but be cynical; he had seen the same business pattern take over everywhere. It was easy to be a manager, he thought. Streamline the business, sell off what isn't profitable, tell the employees they were lucky to have a job and if they couldn't manage twice the work for the same pay they should look somewhere else for employment. That was why the older teachers left and were replaced by graduates straight out of college.

Sadie looked at Paul, a warning signal to tell him to be on his best behaviour. He remembered all too well the last parents' evening. The headmaster had asked one of the new young tech-savvy teachers to give a demonstration of the class monitoring and report system to the parents. The young teacher had the parents playing the role of children, answering quiz questions using tablet computers. Paul had decided to give an answer of 'potato' to the question 'Which fruit is orange and grows on trees?' He'd thought it would be useful to test what would happen if the child was wrong. Unfortunately, the tech-savvy teacher had set up the correct answer program properly but skipped the wrong answer, assuming that the parents would all be able to get such simple questions right. Sceptical about machines, the resulting display had been a joy for Paul to watch. The system had congratulated Paul on his answer with a digital display of fireworks, announcing in a loud digital voice, 'You are correct, a potato is an orange fruit that grows on trees.'

The head teacher, red-faced, had blustered over an explanation, shooting the tech-savvy teacher a look that said 'I'll see you later for an explanation.'

Remembering the incident, Paul looked at Sadie with a mischievous grin. She grabbed his hand and squeezed it.

Louie had dressed for the event. His hair was gelled into a slightly futuristic and geometric take on the dragged-through-a-hedge look. As Louie shook hands with Paul and Sadie, Paul noticed the oversized wristwatch. It was obviously an InfoWatch. On the other wrist, Louie was wearing another device on which a small screen was displaying some kind of continuously scrolling graph. Paul had met Louie last year and had been unimpressed by him.

'Mr and Mrs Clark, please come with me to the hot desk over there.' Louie smiled and gestured to the desk. Paul winced but with Sadie's guiding hand behind his back dutifully crossed the room and arranged the seats for Sadie and himself. Louie smoothed down his new suit jacket and tie and swiped and tapped his left-hand wrist watch. The large screen on the desk responded immediately with an animation which welcomed the parents and then flashed up an animated report of Charlotte's progress. A picture of Charlotte was used as a graph element throughout, stretched on occasions when she had done well and squeezed in subjects in which she performed poorly.

Paul groaned and Sadie gave him a look which he knew all too well. Louie started his narrative as his InfoWatch chipped in with a start signal. His presentation was being timed and controlled by the watch. He chirped in around the progress markers, adding a human touch to the presentation.

'I think Charlotte has most problems in the area of mathematics, science and logic. I notice that she has trouble keeping her watch in working order. We could arrange for her to have a remedial work program if only her watch was working.'

'Yes, we know that Charlotte has problems with the watch. She's an old-fashioned little girl. She has a fascination with books — paper books that is — and she is a little clumsy with technology.' Sadie was almost apologetic.

'It is important in the modern world to be familiar with these technology systems from early on in life,' Louie replied. 'She will need to use these types of systems—'

'Can I ask why a six year old is learning logic?' interrupted a disgruntled Paul.

'Well, we all need a finely tuned critical faculty these days, there's so much charlatanism around every corner.'

'But she's five! She doesn't have a rational logical mind yet; it doesn't develop properly until children are in double figures.'

'Logic is part of the national curriculum, Mr Clark. I am sorry you do not see the importance of the subject. It might be just the thing that saves someone like Charlotte from falling in with the wrong crowd.'

'Sorry, but what exactly do you mean by that?' Paul's look made Louie feel distinctively uncomfortable.

'I mean that there's something of an irrational backlash against the progress of our times . . . modern science, technology, surveillance and so on.'

'By whom?'

'Well, we all know that there have been some sudden changes in society in the last few years and some of these elements are resistant to progress.'

Paul bit his tongue. He knew that if he said what he wanted to say to this teacher Sadie would lose it with him later.

'How is Charlotte doing in the arts?' Paul managed, inwardly congratulating himself on his self-control and strategic change of topic.

'Well, we teach art and drama and as you can see those are the two topics in which Charlotte stands tall.' Pleased with his little joke, Louie gestured towards the graph populated with Charlottes of various heights.

'She likes drama,' Sadie said. 'Charlotte was telling us how she was acting in a play where she had to be a starfish. She loved that, she was drawing starfishes for weeks.' Sadie laughed at the memory of Charlotte trying to pretend her four limbs were really five. She was interrupted by Louie's watch beeping. He had forgotten to set the program to pause while he was dealing with Paul and Sadie's questions and now it had moved on to the next pupil on his list.

'Sorry about this, but we've run out of time.' Louie was slightly flustered. His InfoWatch started chirruping a call to attend to a physiological state warning. He glanced at it briefly, aware of the Clarks watching him. He tapped and swiped at the watch but for some reason the system was frozen and began flashing an alarming shade of red.

'We'll let you get on,' Paul smiled. 'Thanks for your time.' He grabbed Sadie's hand and lifted her to a standing position.

'Okay, er, thanks, you're very welcome.' Louie was trying to hold down three buttons on the watch to force quit and restart.

Paul and Sadie left the classroom. 'Sorry, but I couldn't take any more of that little robot,' Paul said.

'Go easy on him, he's only young and a bit infatuated with the watch.'

'You can see where it's going, can't you? All fluff and no substance. It's ridiculous some of things they teach them — logic for God's sake! I wonder if we should take her out of school and teach her at home.'

Sadie smiled and shook her head. 'Come on, let's get a coffee.'

8

The room was dimly lit and situated in the deepest recesses of the building. ReachOut Informatics had become one of the main players in the data analysis field in the last few years, even providing data to the government under contract. They were one of the centres that handled mass data from the surveillance systems. Most of the data was handled automatically based upon algorithms originally formulated a few years ago, but the analytic team were responsible for looking at specific anomalies in the data.

'This data is getting weirder all the time.'

'What do you mean?'

'I don't know . . . it's almost like it's swinging between two positions.'

'A bimodal distribution?'

'If you combine both samples, yes. But it's as if one sample scores high one day, and the other the next day. It's as if they were swapping habits. But it's not just buying habits, it's physiology . . . well, everything really. Just flip-flopping.'

'Well, look at this data stream that I'm working on — it's showing that size 32 dresses are being bought en masse by size 12 women! Predictions for sales of beekeepers' hats are through the roof and tomato ketchup sales have fallen through the floor. See what I mean? The world's gone mad.'

'I think we need to have a real purge of this data and examine the algorithms again. We might as well stop providing data predictions until this is sorted out. No — we'll go back to averages for this time last year and if they produce a better, more consistent data pattern put the predictions in retrospectively. The weather bureau always gets away with it.'

Just a few doors down the corridor sat a sibyl, conjoined with the computers and quietly sensing an interesting presence outside. At the same time, she sensed another more distant presence making its influence known on the computer-aggregating algorithms. She smiled to herself at the pattern of thin women buying oversized dresses. She liked the sense of comedy in this cyber attack. It didn't take itself too seriously.

Her mind returned to the presence outside. He was still so sure he knew how everything worked. She saw him through the CCTV feed: cocky and argumentative. His name was Louie and he was soon to experience a fall.

She slipped into a dream. She was joined by two other dreamers; she felt their presence and energetics. There was a flash of intuitive recognition between the three, a profound feeling of peace and common intent. Responding to their thoughts, the computers replayed the CCTV footage of Louie for the three of them. They sensed a pattern that was beginning to unfold.

Outside the ReachOut building it was cold. The weak sunlight that had been around that morning had got lost in a progressively cloudy sky the colour of naval battleships. Louie thought it was good they were moving and letting the sun shine through, otherwise they would have been freezing. It was a good turnout, perhaps two hundred or so people, chanting in unison.

'The machine cannot be wrong,
The middle is excluded,
Anecdote is not fact,
In the beginning was chance,
Logic is primary . . .'

Louie felt good among these fellow clear thinkers. In an increasingly technological world, people seemed to be becoming more and more superstitious.

'Woo is not true . . .' His breath billowed like smoke in front of his face.

They held placards emblazoned with 'Woo is not true' and walked up and down on the steps of the building. Mandy and some of the other girls were giving out leaflets and presenting a concise rehearsed argument for the rational point of view. The aim of the demonstration was to systematically argue that notions of intuition were misleading and companies should not use sibyls for business. Louie knew that the government had clamped down and now required any company who wanted to employ a sibyl to obtain a license. It should have meant that the use of sibyls was becoming less common, but that didn't seem to be the case. And it stuck in Louie's throat that some companies and government departments persisted in their use of those fakes.

A car drew up in front of the ReachOut headquarters just a few metres from the demonstration. Two men and a woman got out of the car before it sped off. Louie recognised the tallest of the men as Marvin Goldman, the CEO of ReachOut. He ran over to Goldman, quickly followed by Ron.

'Mr Goldman, can I ask why you use charlatans and frauds in your business?'

Louie ran ahead of Goldman as he paced towards the building.

'Young man, you are stepping close to the line of slander. I would advise you to be careful.'

'But you can't believe that the liminals can really do what you employ them for?'

'All of our employees are carefully selected for their abilities and our personnel department are fully capable of contracting the most appropriate people. Good day.'

'ReachOut is becoming Freakout,' Louie chanted and the rest of the protestors joined in.

Ron had been filming the event and he followed Goldman to the door where security guards pushed him and Louie away from the entrance back onto the steps.

Louie turned to Ron. 'Let's try and get in through the back.'

Before following Louie, Ron waved his wristwatch in the direction of the demonstrators. The action transmitted a simple message to the context-prioritised members of his contacts book. Ron ran after Louie, his trenchcoat tails flapping uncontrollably around his legs. He had to stop twice to untangle them. Turning, Louie saw Ron bending down and extracting himself from black leather. He rolled his eyes heavenwards. 'Come on, Ron!'

Louie found the door easily and tapped a sequence into the keypad on the lock. He pushed the door and it opened. Ron looked at Louie quizzically, impressed that he had known the entrance code. Four of the protestors followed Louie and Ron into what looked like a storage room.

They had no plan but Louie seemed to know what he was doing. He headed through a door at the end of the room and up a metal staircase. At the first floor landing, he hesitated and then continued up the stairs. They followed him up five flights of stairs before he stopped and went through a door.

They found themselves in a long bare corridor. Louie ran down the corridor and stopped in front of a black door labelled Communications. There was a light with a blue pulsing glow situated above the door. Louie stood in front of it entranced; it seemed somehow familiar to him. The door had another keypad lock. He confidently tapped in six numbers and there was the sound of the lock disengaging. Now Louie looked as astonished as Ron and the others. He turned to look at them all and then slowly urged the door open.

There was a blue glow penetrating the darkness, pulsing faintly like the one over the entrance door. His eyes adapted slowly as he moved further into the room. He could see a bank of glowing screens surrounding a circular framework. In the centre of the orb was a young woman in a large reclining seat. Wires issued from the figure-hugging suit and helmet that she wore, connecting her to the mechanism and the computers beyond. Louie stared. He couldn't believe his luck. He had managed to access the inner sanctum, the place where the sibyls worked. Everybody knew the way the system worked, at least in principle. The sibyl was at the centre of a rich network of digital communications intuitively sorting data. She generated an emotional attractor which was used to orient and direct the company's online presence. These were machines integrated with the human mind. Louie was impressed to see the technology for the first time. What he didn't like was the psychic aspect, the notion that the sibyl was able to intuit from the sensory data being fed to her what might happen next. Definitely woo!

The screens around the orb that held the seated sibyl flashed up a video stream of Louie. It was obviously him but he looked a little more dishevelled; his beard had gone and he had lost his smart trending urban look. The framework turned towards them. The sibyl was staring at them through a tinted visor. He couldn't see her eyes but he felt them in some strange way. A young female voice spoke and was amplified by the public address system in the room.

'Welcome, Louie.'

The screens continued to show a video of Louie, but now in the picture he too had a headset on like a sibyl.

Ron was astounded, mouth open. They all looked at Louie, who was staring aghast at the image of himself on the screen. He felt suddenly hot. He found himself staring at the sibyl, transfixed. The sibyl was speaking again.

'Louie, this is for you only. Your destiny is with us, not with your companions.'

Louie looked at Ron. 'Did you hear that?' he demanded. Ron shook his head.

'Louie, I said it is for you only. Your friends cannot hear me because I am not speaking. What a conundrum for you!'

'Did you hear that?' Louie asked, shaking.

Ron and the others shook their heads and looked at Louie pityingly.

Louie was afire. He began to feel the pulsing light in his hands and fingertips. He looked at the sibyl in the centre and began to feel as if he was in her place. The screens showed him donning the helmet and visor that the sibyl wore.

51

He turned from the images and sped out of the room. His steps rang out on the metal staircase as he took the stairs three at a time. Ron and the others followed. When they reached the entrance door downstairs the security guards were already there. As soon as they came through the door, they were corralled into a spot by the wall. 'You can't hold us,' Ron shouted. 'We haven't done anything!'

He looked around for Louie, but Louie was nowhere to be seen.

PART TWO

ALL CHANGE

9

Paul was partly listening to some music and partly flicking through a book on dreams. He had always been fascinated by the richness and complexity of dreams. The intelligence that created these inner dramas was incredibly impressive. They were a concoction of the real, the assumed and the fantastical. He knew that some dreams came out of anxiety — the typical dream of being late for school or work — or out of a desire for the unobtainable. But beyond this theatre of the mundane was the archetypal dream. The psychologist Carl Jung had called them 'big dreams'. These were messages for the many. Jung had noticed in the years leading up to The First World War that many of his patients were having dreams that seemed to suggest a bloody catastrophe was well on the way. Jung had had his own vision — like a waking dream — on a rail journey in October 1913, when he saw a catastrophic sea overwhelm northern Europe. The sea became blood-coloured and the mountains of Switzerland grew to protect the country from the flood.

Paul heard a commotion and looked up towards the kitchen. Sadie was cooking. Charlotte was shouting, 'More sugar, more sugar!' There would be flour everywhere; there always was when Charlotte helped to bake.

He looked down at the book in his hands. Modern interpretations of dreams had become ever more mechanical.

Dreams were too often seen as just a means for the brain to record, sort and store information, just as a computer in sleep mode tidies up the data stored on the hard drive. In his opinion, it was a poverty-stricken explanation. The dreams he was seeing in his practice were not just about laying down tidy memories. They were an announcement that something was coming.

Carla had given him a great example. She had seen in her dreams thousands of people standing in a large square surrounded by ornate buildings. While they stood there, not talking or moving, their shadows seemed to wrench themselves loose of the bodies they belonged to and moved around on their own. The shadows made mischief, climbed the building facades, swapped places, and danced around before running off en masse out of the square. In the now blazing sunlight the people stood without shadows, like statues staring into the distance with no impetus of their own. A shadow was something you didn't think about, but if it wasn't there, you would notice its eerie absence.

He heard a screech and ducked to avoid Charlotte's floury-fingered grasp. She grimaced with a comical demonic expression, threatening fingers held up like claws covered with almond pastry filling. She growled and lunged as Paul swept her off her feet and grabbed her hand. He licked her fingers, tasting the almond filling, and feigned a faint caused by the magical mix. Charlotte giggled.

The phone rang. Paul put Charlotte down and she ran back into the kitchen licking her fingers.

'Hello? Yes, that's right I do . . . Yes, I've heard about that. Yes, I agree, that would be very interesting. Yes, I do have time. I could do that. That's fine, look forward to seeing you then.'

He wandered into the kitchen. Sadie looked like she been through an explosion. She had cake mix on her cheek and icing sugar and flour in her hair.

'Who was that?' she asked.

'It was a Dr Marsden . . . an anthropologist. He wants to meet up about some project.'

'What project?' Sadie dusted down her apron.

'I'm not sure entirely, something about dreams. We're meeting on Wednesday morning.'

'Sounds intriguing,' Sadie said. 'Now, who wants to lick this bowl?'

Louie watched the changing displays on his watch. The display was flashing red alert on nearly all his physiological measures. He felt there was no other option: he unclasped his watch, slipped the back off and removed the battery. As long as it had power, it was tracking his whereabouts and sending the details back to his service provider and God knows who else.

At home, he packed some things and headed straight back out. The experience with the sibyl had shaken him profoundly. She had said he was one of them. What the hell did that mean? Why couldn't his friends hear the message? It was probably good that they hadn't. He couldn't face talking to Ron or Mandy right now. He needed time on his own to try to figure out what was happening. The demonstration had not shaken ReachOut as planned; instead, his contact with the sibyl had shaken him up completely.

He felt he had to get out of London. At King's Cross he bought a ticket to go north. There was an awkward moment at the gate because he didn't buy a digital ticket with his watch; instead he had insisted on a printed paper ticket. The young guard was only used to older folks having paper tickets and he looked at Louie suspiciously.

The train, bound for Edinburgh, was due to leave in ten minutes. Louie bundled into a forward-facing seat with his rucksack and some supplies: crisps and a cellophane sealed sandwich he had bought in the station. He automatically went to look at his watch, and found himself searching up his sleeve for it before remembering that it was in his bag. It had been years since he had removed the watch, he felt naked without it. He had even worn it while he slept. As he sat waiting for the train to pull out, he absentmindedly looked again at his wrist three or four times before pushing his left hand down with his right, as if it had its own intentions, à la Dr Strangelove.

The train was quiet and no one had chosen to sit near Louie.

He was dishevelled, and his watch-checking made him look like he had a nervous tic, as he raised his arm occasionally and then swore at himself under his breath. As the train snaked through the suburbs, Louie surveyed the almost empty carriage. A few seats down, a older couple sat with a grandchild who was playing on a tablet computer. The child was being cheered every time he killed a small digital pig. Near them, two businessmen and a woman were discussing marketing and the use of proprietary data catchment and social networks.

A girl walked down the aisle. Louie tried not to meet her gaze. She was dressed in an old bag lady overcoat coming apart at the seams. She wore long thick brown socks connecting tatty trainers to a long woollen skirt. A purple hoody was visible under her coat and as she settled into the seat opposite Louie, she lowered the hood to reveal a confident smile and a pair of dark, dark eyes. She looked at her watch and he noticed that it was not an InfoWatch but an antique clockwork piece on a thick brown leather strap, almost military in style.

He was sure she was a sibyl, but she did not dress in the usual dark clothes and she did not have the tendency to avoid people's gaze. Instead, she met his surreptitious glance and smiled at him broadly. Shit! It was going to be a pain in the arse having to sit with a liminal all the way to Scotland. Although, he thought, she might not go all the way.

He automatically went to look at his watch, which wasn't there, and cursed his actions under his breath.

She looked at him sympathetically. 'Tourette's?'

'What?'

'I see you suffer from Tourette's syndrome,' she said.

'Fuck off!'

Surprised himself by his outburst, Louie hastily apologised. For some reason, her comments irked him. He checked his wrist again and made a raspberry sound as he tried to stifle the words coming out of his mouth.

She smiled again.

'Better out than in.'

Louie blushed slightly and tried looking out of the window

at the passing scenery. The montage of rusty buildings, damp greenery and occasional fly tip focused his thoughts. He couldn't believe that people would gather up their garden rubbish — sometimes household rubbish like the odd sofa — and just deposit it over the fence that separated their garden from the railway embankment. It was definitely a case of out of sight out of mind.

Her words broke through the silence.

'I'm Swallow. Where are you going?'

He turned to look at her. That perpetual smile was irritating.

'Swallow?'

'Yes. Hippy parents, I'm afraid. I was lucky really, my brother was named Tree.'

The smile seemed to be there even when she moved her mouth to speak.

'Tree?'

'Are you monosyllabic?' She shrugged. 'I suppose it helps with the stutter.'

'I am not fuh-fuh-f-king suffering from f-king Tourette's and I do n-n-not have a fucking st—stutter.'

She smiled that irksome smile.

Louie tried to calm down. He wondered whether he should move seats, and began to reach for his bag.

The elderly couple were glaring down the carriage at him. He heard them trying to explain to their grandson what Tourette's syndrome was.

She was off again, 'You didn't say where you're going?'

Just tell her and get it over with, he thought. Then he would move seats.

'Scotland — Edinburgh.'

'Me too. How exciting. I'm returning after a couple of weeks in London.'

He tried to ignore her and rested his head against the window. The blur of the passing landscape disappeared as his eyes closed and he drifted off, thinking about his experiences of the last few days.

He found himself in quicksand. He tried to walk but his legs wouldn't move him. Now he was sinking into the quicksand. It occurred to him that movement was supposed to make you sink faster, so he stopped struggling and looked around him. Spotting a branch not too far away, he stretched for it, moving ever so slightly closer to a horizontal position. If he could lie flat, maybe he could pull himself to the edge . . .

He saw a movement at the edge of the pool and turned to look. Swallow was standing on the bank watching him. Next to her was another girl sitting on a rock. The other girl had blond hair and bright blue eyes. She smiled at Louie and it was a glorious smile. She reached out to him and he grasped her hand. She seemed to have tremendous strength because he was pulled out of the quicksand almost instantaneously.

Louie woke, but for a moment he thought he was still in the dream. The girl who had rescued him was sitting next to Swallow in the seat opposite. He stared through half-closed eyes for a while and then finally dared to open them. As he did so both Swallow and this new arrival stopped talking to each other and stared at Louie.

'You have a little drool hanging from the side of your mouth,' Swallow smiled broadly.

His hand moved quickly to his mouth.

'You don't really, she's a tease,' the blond girl said.

'You're real,' he thought, but the words had already slipped out.

The blond girl pinched herself, feigned pain and nodded.

'He's been dreaming of you, how sweet.'

'Give it up, Swallow, he's getting embarrassed.'

'I did have a dream,' Louie said, 'and you were in it — or someone like you.'

'Maybe you opened your eyes partially and subliminally saw me during your doze, then you incorporated the image into your dream,' the blond girl said.

'It's possible.'

'Sure it's possible, everything is possible. If you carry on reasoning it out maybe you can explain it away completely.'

'What do you mean?' Louie exclaimed.

'Sometimes that little bit of uncertainty is good to hold on to. There is a little point of magic there.'

'A little point?' Swallow asked, looking serious. 'Like an atom?'

The blond girl smiled.

'A molecule? A boson?' Swallow went on, warming to her subject.

'Enough!' The blond girl was smiling but her tone was firm.

'Just trying to be helpful.' Swallow looked a little peeved.

The blond girl turned to Louie.

'My name is Zara. I'm a friend of Swallow's. Have some food Louie . . . you need to gather your wits together.' Her voice was authoritative but her face exuded kindness.

He took his sandwich and crisps out of his bag without question and peeled back the cellophane.

There was a knock at the door and Paul opened it to encounter a tall man who looked to be in his sixties.

'Dr Clark I presume? I am Alan Marsden.'

'Pleased to meet you,' answered Paul. He showed Marsden into the office. Marsden looked around with interest.

'I've never actually seen a working psychologist's office. Academics, of course, but not someone actually practising psychoanalysis.'

He took a good look at the couch, made comfortable with blankets and cushions. It looked like the classic image of the couch in Freud's office museum.

'It's only a small room but it helps to focus the mind,' Paul said.

'Can I?' Marsden looked at Paul and then at the couch. Paul smiled at his request.

'Of course, feel free.'

Marsden positioned his large frame on the couch and made himself comfortable.

'Don't worry, I don't need analysis. It's just so evocative.'

'What can I do for you, Dr Marsden?'

'Well I'm hoping to interest you in a mutually beneficial

project.' He put his hands behind his head.

'Oh?'

'I recently heard about your involvement with Charlotte Mendes. You treated her, is that right?'

Paul was surprised to hear Charlotte's name mentioned. 'Yes. I was asked to help out at the hospital but it turned out to be much more involved than I could have imagined.'

'Yes, interesting, very interesting. I am familiar with some of the issues. I have been making a study of the so-called sibyls . . . from an anthropological view of course. But I expect that, as a psychologist, you would agree that there are areas of overlap.'

'Of course.'

'Can I ask you what you think is happening with these individuals? Perhaps I should make it clear that I am sympathetic to their plight.'

Paul was surprised at Marsden's request and his straightforwardness. He had never spoken to anyone this frankly about the sibyls.

'Well, I would say that the phenomenon is usually restricted to young females and that they have unusually developed intuitive capacities. In some extreme cases — such as Charlotte's — this seems to also include a kind of hypnotic control over people and possibly a psychokinetic influence over objects around them.'

'Fascinating.' Marsden pulled himself up to a seated position on the couch to listen.

'As a result of these unusual abilities, they tend to be marginalised,' Paul continued. 'The numbers of sibyls seem to be increasing and they're fast being used as scapegoats by the governments and corporations. It's almost becoming a witch -hunt.'

'Exactly! My thoughts exactly. As an anthropologist you see these kinds of abilities attributed to certain people, such as shamans, healers and other marginal figures. These people are often shunned, they live apart from the majority and the people are wary of them. They go to them when they need help but otherwise they stay well away. Traditionally, these people — shall we call them wise women or men? — pass on their knowledge to a suitable apprentice before they die and so there is a line of similar individuals, but only one practising at any time in a community of course. What is interesting with the sibyls is the numbers, the sheer numbers.' Marsden stared into space, lost in his own thoughts for a moment.

'Do you have any idea why we've seen so many of them in the last few years?' Paul asked. Since Charlotte's death it seemed like he saw clones of her everywhere. It was unnerving but he was having to get used to it.

'I have wondered about this myself,' Marsden said. He frowned and seemed to be incubating a thought. He turned his head to look intently at Paul.

'If I were pushed to identify a single factor I would say it is the machines. People are depending on technology more than ever before. The machines are recording every facet of their daily life. Heart rate, diet, walking pace, shopping choices, when to have dreams, when to wake up, who they should have relationships with. In effect, the machines have taken over. The mind has found itself freed — but to do what? The rational mind has become mechanised; the more intuitive, unconscious aspect of the mind has been freed to redevelop older capacities. Essentially, we are seeing a rebirth of the mythological mind. I am not sure where this will take us. One thing is guaranteed — the transition is not going to go smoothly.'

'I think you're right,' replied Paul. 'I favour the idea that we have two aspects to our thinking: a rational aspect and a more experiential aspect which is more intuitive, and relates more to creativity and dreams. Normally these two types of mind work together harmoniously, but as you say we have entered a time where there seems to be a rift between the two. Increasingly, the mind's rational functions have been replaced by machines. As a consequence, the experiential aspect has grown to compensate. It is of course the experiential aspect that is responsible for the kinds of phenomena we attribute to the sibyls . . . Why do you say it's not going to go smoothly?' Marsden spoke with a gravity that demanded attention.

'The machine is the model for the rational mind, but it is

an aberration. It is the ideal of the human mind, stripped of emotions and morality. The experiential mind, as you call it — I like the term by the way — is nested in nature, it derives from the body. The rational mind is the best and worst aspect of humans. When it gets detached from the experiential, it loses its connection to the whole and becomes selfish, devious, possibly psychopathic. Ultimately, encouraging the dominance of the machine is a program for selfish ends. I believe that a return to the experiential, to the natural, must happen but it won't occur without some friction.'

'Dr Marsden—'

'Please call me Alan.'

'Alan . . . I'm intrigued by your ideas.'

'Good, good. The reason I wanted to meet with you is to talk about dreaming. I gave a talk to a learned society a few days ago. I was heckled by a few young people who I would say were devotees of the machine. You know the type, little hard-liners, constantly checking their InfoWatches and promoting the benefits of the mind-as-a-machine metaphor, only — sadly — they think it is real. Anyway, the curious thing was that I had already seen what transpired at the talk a week earlier in a dream. The young man was exactly the same as the one in my dream, the way he looked and even what he said.'

Paul leaned forward to focus on Marsden's words.

'I've had a number of people telling me that their dreams have been forecasting the future. I had a client, a young woman, who specifically told me that she thought her dreams were becoming reality.'

'Was she a sibyl?'

'Yes . . . high functioning, holding down a freelance job and otherwise psychologically sound.'

'Interesting, interesting.'

'I ruled out self-deception. She really is convinced that she's dreaming things that happen a short time later. Your dream was accurate compared to the real event?'

Marsden nodded. 'Absolutely. Very accurate.'

'It appears that these predictive dreams often seem to involve some future contact with a sibyl. Although the characters at your talk don't sound like sibyls . . .'

10

Louie had been on the train for two hours and they were halfway to Edinburgh. He had fallen quiet and Swallow and Zara had dozed off themselves, or at least they sat with their eyes closed. His mind drifted back to the events earlier that day. He hadn't really had time to think through what had happened. It all seemed unreal now, as dramatic events often do after the fact. He had run from the ReachOut building because he couldn't believe what had happened. He hated sibyls — they were the epitome of the kind of thinking he had devoted his life to undermining. Humans were woolly-headed enough but sibyls . . . they were evolutionary throwbacks, flotsam and jetsam from the premodern past.

The sibyl's comments about him had been so embarrassing; he felt humiliated and went slightly red just remembering her words. She had labelled him a sibyl. Perhaps Ron and the others now did too. It had to be a mistake — or perhaps she was playing mind games with him. But then how had he known the door pad codes? How did he know which rooms to go to? It had all seemed familiar somehow, almost as if he had been there before. The sibyl who had called him by name, she was familiar too. Even in the moment, when he'd been listening to her words with horror, he had felt a connection, some kind of sharing deep down. It didn't make sense. Louie felt he was in uncharted territory and lacked the words to explain or understand what had happened.

He felt uneasy even now. He wasn't sure what was going on with Swallow and Zara. The dream he'd had with Zara in it had been odd. Perhaps it was just as they said; his eyes had flickered open briefly and his dream had incorporated Zara's image. He knew this was a reasonable explanation. He had often heard his watch alarm when sleeping and incorporated the sounds into his dream imagery.

He stole a look at Zara. He had met her only an hour ago, discounting the time in the dream, but he felt he'd known her forever. Her face was angelic, her complexion perfect. Even though the deep blue eyes were now closed, he imagined he could still see and feel that gaze. He couldn't believe how he had felt talking to her.

Louie didn't believe in love at first sight, it was complete bunkum, the highest level of woolly thinking. His previous relationships had been arranged through perfect profile matching. A multidimensional personality profile was uploaded from his InfoWatch and he was offered a list of possible matches. None of them had worked out but he attributed that to poor data quality. It was likely that the candidates had not been honest when they had finalised their profile. Now he was captured by this unknown and unquantified girl.

Zara opened her eyes, catching sight of Louie staring at her, lost in his thoughts. She smiled. Louie was startled; he hadn't noticed that her eyes had opened.

He returned her smile gingerly.

'Why don't you come with us?'

'I'm sorry?'

'I said, why don't you come with us? You don't have anywhere specific to go, do you?'

'I hardly know you.'

'You can get to know me.' Her smile was irresistible. 'We're going back to our aunt's; she has a smallholding in Aberdeenshire. You would be very welcome there.'

'Well . . . I don't know how long I'm going be in Scotland.'

'Well . . .' Zara mirrored Louie's cadence and emphasis exactly. 'Come for a little while.'

She held his gaze and Louie could feel himself gravitating to her request. He really wasn't sure why; it seemed preposterous. He was the kind of person who liked to plan things out carefully and in detail, but now it seemed that his normally organised life was giving way to chance and fortune.

'Deacon wants us to report to him tomorrow about the data collection issues.'

Schulz stood tall, gazing down at Frobisher who was sitting at his desk.

'I think the liminals are rapidly growing in numbers.' Frobisher leaned back in his chair and threaded his long fingers together into a comfortable clasp over his solar plexus.

'We are still talking minorities though . . . little groups and individuals,' Schulz said, sinking down into the leather upholstered chair opposite Frobisher.

'But we have a seen a real surge in the numbers of liminals since the Mendes event,' Frobisher said. 'If you remember, they were real minorities before that time. Then it all changed, and now there are hundreds of thousands under mandatory monitoring, and I suspect many more out of the net entirely. We need better monitoring; I always thought we should make the watches irremovable. I think he is ready to consider such developments.'

'What are we going to do about the data collection?' Schulz asked. 'It's been producing some very strange patterns lately. The corporations have started fining us for inaccurate data prediction.'

'Well, we know there are centres of insurgence. We should look into identifying them and detain the operators, permanently if necessary.'

'Orange jumpsuits?'

'Implants!' Frobisher said with relish.

'It would certainly ensure good, accurate data retrieval.'

'Exactly.'

71

'These are acts of terrorism, they need to be dealt with accordingly.'

'We can push for a stricter response to the liminals,' Frobisher said. 'We need more control before they poison society with their nonsense. But we'll keep this undocumented for now in case of any leaks. Slowly, slowly, catchy monkey.'

The cat's sinuous walk was pure poetry. It took a leap to the ground, absorbing the momentum by crouching low to the floor before rising up again on furry shock absorbers.

'Abigail, get out of the way.'

The cat moved lithely to the side and looked up at Agnes with a quizzical expression. Agnes opened the door to the outhouse to view the cages. Two Bengal cats were sitting on a platform at head height, purring loudly. They were obviously temporarily satisfied with their lot. Another cat in the next cage was pushing a small plastic food bowl up the side of the cage, pressing it against the mesh and pushing with her paws so that it slowly rose. Agnes smiled. These cats were agile but completely nuts, barely domesticated. She had fallen in love with them because of their unwillingness to toe the line. The smallholding had acquired a cosmopolitan mix of waifs and strays, the cats not least.

She turned for a moment to look at the farmyard and then past it to the fields and the wooded hills beyond. Over the centuries, these lands had sheltered many who had fled the system and sought anonymity in this wild country.

The smallholding was about half a mile from the road and the road itself was another two miles from any reasonable thoroughfare. She liked the silence here; it was peaceful in a way she had never experienced before moving here five years ago.

From here she had a good view of the yard and the lane which led to the public road. Strolling into the farmyard were Swallow and Zara, with a young man in tow. Agnes had been expecting them. She had seen the young man in her dreams . . . or had she made him in her dreams? He looked younger than she remembered from her dream, but it was definitely him.

'Agnes, this is Louie. Louie, Agnes.'

'Pleased to meet you, Louie.'

'Likewise.'

Louie felt awkward but stretched out his hand to shake Agnes's.

Swallow mumbled something under her breath about civilising the little runt at last. Agnes caught it and flicked a stern but humorous glance at Swallow.

'Come in, come in, it is cold.'

They passed through a wooden porch, laden with clematis, into the house. Agnes' house was an old stone cottage, whitewashed in the vernacular. The rooms were on the small side but they were cosy. They had come straight into what Louie assumed was the main living room. The stone floor was covered with large Turkish rugs in bright jewel-like patterns and colours. The room was dominated by a huge inglenook fire which was burning fast, casting dancing flames up the large chimney. Louie felt the warmth immediately. He had never seen a real fire in his life and he found it difficult to draw his attention away from it.

'Well, we should have some tea and oaties to warm you up, what do you say, Louie?'

'Yes, thank you, that would be good.'

Louie was still unsure how he had ended up here. Looking at Agnes, he decided that she couldn't possibly be Swallow and Zara's aunt. Agnes was obviously Chinese, even if she did have a strong Scottish accent.

Swallow and Zara sat together on a well-stuffed sofa while Louie settled into a big leather chair near the fire. He stared at the logs, which were now settling to a steady flurry of flames. He found himself liking this room; it was very simply furnished and decorated.

'Here you are, try these. I made them this morning.' Agnes placed some oatcakes on the table in the centre of the room and deposited a large blue teapot and four cups next to them.

Swallow reached across and picked up an oatcake.

'Mmm, real food. We've missed this.'

Agnes smiled and urged Louie to try one while she poured the tea. Louie had never eaten an oatcake and gingerly tasted it. The oatcake's powdery texture crumbled and then melted in his mouth with a salty, buttery aftertaste. They were delicious and he reached back to the plate and took another two, feeling suddenly ravenous. Agnes and the girls laughed.

Later, Agnes showed him to a room under the eaves with a sloping ceiling and a polished wooden floor. Through a tiny casement window he could glimpse the stars. With no artificial light for miles around he could even make out the shape of the Milky Way.

That night, Louie slept well and woke up early the next morning. Unusually for him, he found that he could easily remember his dreams. He dreamt that he had been back in London, and was trying to explain himself to Ron and Mandy. The dream left him feeling uncomfortable that he had left his friends in the way he did. He was still at a loss as to why he had found his way so easily in the ReachOut headquarters. He had never before run away from a situation like that but the message from the sibyl had thoroughly unnerved him. Meeting Swallow and Zara and ending up in Scotland at this out-of-the-way place had been the pinnacle of a completely absurd day. He told himself that the farm was perhaps a useful place to hide out a for a day or two but he couldn't imagine it being a long-term stay. At the same time, he felt a strange but not unwelcome urge to spend more time with Zara. This just wasn't like him.

He tried to put her out of his thoughts and see things from a more rational perspective. Perhaps he had fallen on his feet after all. He had a strong suspicion that Zara and Swallow, and perhaps Agnes too, were liminals. If so, he had found himself in a little hotbed of subversives. Exactly the kind of place he had always dreamt of infiltrating. This was a great opportunity to out them all, to reveal them to be the irrational types they were. Maybe he was the one to bring a hard shot of logic to their woolly little world.

11

He left his room and went downstairs to the main house. He was beginning to find this house impossible to navigate. From the outside it looked like an old stone cottage, but inside, room after room led off dark unlit corridors. It seemed that a number of outbuildings had been attached to the main building and further extensions made to these. He followed a corridor which he thought led to the living room they were in yesterday, only to find himself back in the kitchen. He was standing there puzzled when Zara walked up behind him. He jumped when she tapped him on the shoulder.

'Good morning, Louie.'

'Oh, hi. I think I'm lost . . . I was looking for the living room we were in yesterday.'

'Yes, the house is something of a maze, isn't it? We should go outside and look at where we are and then you can meet some of the others.'

She surprised him by taking his hand. She led him back down the corridor he had just walked along and through two rooms to an outside courtyard. The building looked different again from this perspective. From the courtyard, the house looked more like a nineteenth century coach house, with spaces for horses and storerooms for equipment. There were old roses hanging from the walls and the perfume was strong, sweet and intoxicating with a slight aroma of jasmine.

Zara led him across the courtyard and through double doors to a large square of grass outside. The sunlight was bright now and through bleary eyes he could see human shapes moving on the grass beneath what looked like fruit trees. They seemed to be engaged in a slow-moving dance, or perhaps a kind of martial arts display. He could see Swallow and ten or so others, mostly female but with a couple of men among them. He tried to count them, but each time he came up with a different number. The light was unique, piercing the little orchard and throwing rich shadows across the grass.

Zara continued to hold his hand.

'Can you see what they are doing?' she asked.

'They seem to be doing Tai Chi.'

'Close. They are collecting light . . . the light is essential to dreaming.'

'What do you mean? This sounds like gobbly-de-gook to me.' He let her hand go, then regretted losing touch.

'It's a way of speaking but it's not literal,' Zara said, laughing at his discomfort. 'Louie, you will find that these kinds of ideas are difficult to entertain if your thinking is too literal. Some of the tasks that we are working on almost require throwing the literal mind overboard. Flotsam and jetsam, as it were.'

She said the phrase in such a way that it seemed to have a particular relevance to her. Louie looked at her curiously. He found it hard to believe he was standing here listening to this. If it was anyone else spouting this kind of nonsense he would dismiss it immediately. Instead, he found himself asking a question.

'What do you mean by dreaming?'

'If you're looking for definitions you'll be disappointed. These things stem from the body as a whole, and the normal mind has little leverage at all on these issues.'

'You must be able to tell me what it is in some form. If you can't articulate an idea clearly then there really is a problem.' Louie was surprised at his own irritation. At the same time, he realised that he felt calmer than he usually did. If he'd been somewhere else he probably would have exploded in a fit of hyper-rationalism by now.

Zara turned to him. He got the impression that she was aware of what he was thinking. She smiled, and the last few remnants of his irritation evaporated, suddenly no longer important as she reached for his hand again.

'Dreaming is a movement of the body–mind — like everything else is — but it faces a different direction to the world in which the person is currently in. By taking a different stance, it becomes part of another world which faces the same way. See, easy!'

Louie's expression suggested that he was no better off. He gazed at Zara as if waiting for some kind of clarification. She stared back at him in complete silence and he focused on the warmth of her hand in his.

It suddenly began to seem to Louie that he was watching a film with jerky celluloid frames flashing through the lens of an old projector. Zara seemed to blink on and off, and then was completely gone as if the film had snapped. He wanted to turn and look for her but he couldn't move; his feet were fixed to the earth he stood on and he couldn't even move his head to look to the side. The fingers of his now empty hand prickled and he started to hyperventilate as it occurred to him that he was probably having some kind of attack. As he panicked, the fixation ended and he found himself bent over, vomiting on the grass. Zara stood over him, rubbing his back and asking if he was all right.

They walked back to the house. They found Agnes in the kitchen and she placed some tea and warm bread rolls down on the table for them. Louie breathed in the scent of freshly baked bread; the aroma focused his mind but didn't settle his stomach and he felt like he was going to vomit again. Agnes gently held his hands and ran her thumbs up his wrists, pressing gently in a relaxing and soothing rhythm between the two central tendons.

'I wonder if it's better for him to have food first, before showing him dreaming, Zara?'

'Yes, I think you're right.'

'What happened?' Louie was still a little light-headed but was starting to feel better.

'It's okay, you just needed some food. Have a little to eat and drink and you'll feel fine.' Agnes emphasised the words and finished rubbing his wrists. Louie slowly chewed a morsel of the bread and sipped his tea.

'Agnes, I think we need to explain things to Louie don't we?'

'Yes, it can be difficult getting to grips with the concepts we work with.'

'It is a lot to take in, Louie. But you need to put aside your scepticism. This world is more like a dream than you think.'

Instead of provoking the usual rational backlash from him, Louie found that there was something about the way Zara had delivered her words that left him very relaxed and slightly dreamy himself.

He managed to mutter, 'Okay.'

'If you enter into this world then your mind will make the necessary changes and you won't have as many adverse reactions. Just try to relax into it; it will come.'

Zara treated him to one of her dazzling smiles and he found himself grinning back at her like an idiot.

Frobisher and Schulz walked through the double doors into Deacon's office to find him sitting behind his dark wooden desk. The desk was clear and the highly polished wooden surface shone brilliantly. There was a photograph of Deacon's family on the left corner of the desk and a small brass and copper horary in motion on the right. The little planets rotated in dainty, jerky little orbits around a yellow plastic sun. Frobisher and Schulz took two chairs facing Deacon and sat down.

'Sir, we need to bring to your attention more irregularities in the data capture.'

'Indeed.'

There was an uncomfortable silence which Schulz and Frobisher, as always, felt a growing need to fill. This was Deacon's usual form of conversation. He would fill the gap himself shortly but not until everyone felt slightly uncomfortable.

'Why is that?'

Frobisher and Schulz stopped holding their breath and looked visibly relieved that they could fill the silence again themselves.

'We think, sir, that some organised liminal groups are deliberately transmitting false data. The patterns just do not make sense and when the data has been allowed to go through into the guiding programs and is broadcasted back it's creating confusion. We have now isolated most of the erroneous signals and ensured the broadcast is purer.' Frobisher finished speaking and felt an urgent desire to scratch his right ear.

'Good,' Deacon offered.

Here it came again, Frobisher and Schulz thought, the dreadful pause. Frobisher began silently counting . . . one, two, three . . . ten.

'We do need to address these issues. What do you suggest?' Deacon said.

'Well, we thought we might seek further legislation to ensure that the liminals cannot remove their watches,' Frobisher said.

'Did you indeed?' Deacon ruminated on how precocious these subordinates were becoming under his patronage.

Frobisher began counting, but Schulz pushed on, forgetting the ten second rule.

'Or perhaps we could—'

'Ahem.' Deacon cleared his throat and simultaneously cut off Schulz mid-sentence.

'What would that look like to people?' Deacon's question was rhetorical. 'At the same time,' he mused, 'we cannot allow minorities to upset progress. What we need is a situation where the people find the minorities intolerable. A series of . . . events that indicate that the liminals are upsetting the order of things and are a clear and present danger to the society that we know and love. I hope that we understand each other.'

Frobisher and Schulz nodded in unison.

'I never said this, and I don't want to know how you act on this,' Deacon continued. 'I lead this department, but you understand that I cannot take responsibility for this kind of action. But you can be sure that if we are successful in doing this, there will be rewards for those who got their hands dirty.'

Frobisher and Schulz were clearly excited about having the chance to hit back at the sibyls. But from what Deacon had said, it was clear that they would be the ones to carry the can if things went wrong.

Deacon watched them leave the room. He had noticed while they were talking that the small monitor on his desk, which showed their real-time physiological states, was peaking in the red on the psychopathic and sociopathic scales. The two of them were half-wits but they excelled in psychopathy. Just what was needed: expendables. He'd learnt that the first principle of being a leader was to use those around you and their talents. Psychopaths tended to climb the ladder easily and nothing ever got under their skin, providing them with a somewhat illusory sense of invulnerability.

He had a keen recognition for another psychopathic personality. It takes one to know one, he thought. Most businesses and organisations had a nucleus of psychopaths and sociopaths somewhere in the hierarchy. It was ironic, he thought, how these people could form a nucleus when they were ultimately always out for themselves, but they did. Perhaps this was why corporations had become psychopathic themselves. Deacon admired the way that Big Pharma had commonly sold drugs that hadn't been tested properly, and advertised them 'off label' for uses they weren't designed for. Essentially, they had managed to increase their already obscene profits and turn illness into a universal state, so that everyone needed medicating for something or other. If that wasn't psychopathic behaviour what was? It amused him that corporations might be places where psychopaths could prosper. He was looking forward to his future appointment as a director of AltaHealth when he had finished this round of government. He already had some novel ideas about sowing the seeds of certain illnesses that the company would then produce the panacea for.

He packed his briefcase, mulling over the future potential of improbable pandemics. He checked his diary for tomorrow with his secretary then decided to go home early.

The room was silent, not even the sound of a bird outside could be heard. There were twenty sibyls in the room, all sitting cross-legged on the floor at equally spaced intervals. Their heads were lowered, hands resting on laps. The room had the feel of a Buddhist temple, but the sibyls weren't in Nirvana, they were dream-making.

Louie looked down on them from the small mezzanine floor above. He could see Zara and Swallow. As he watched, he felt himself becoming quieter and calmer, his mind drifting slowly like a leaf on a small stream.

He suddenly found himself walking alone in a forest. The trees towered above him, reaching for a bright sunlit sky. Each footfall was strange, almost like he was stepping onto sponge and each step sinking, cushioned. The air seemed thick. It felt like he was breathing water, cool and fresh, penetrating deep inside. Even his feet felt like they were involved in each breath.

He carried on walking, becoming accustomed to the strange feeling. The forest soon came to an end and the landscape beyond was completely different. Curiously and unexpectedly, there was now desert sand reaching to the horizon. He climbed a dune and saw an oasis, perhaps a mile or so away. He headed towards it. Closing in on the oasis, he saw trees encircling a waterhole and tethered animals. A cluster of tents was pitched around the water, their fabric billowing gently in the breeze. He walked along the water's edge, and again the silence captured him. He had not felt so at ease ever in his life. Every moment seemed to stretch out effortlessly and infinitely; he felt as if he could ride this moment forever.

He walked towards what seemed to be the largest tent. The door flap was already open. Ducking through the doorway he came upon the dreaming group of sibyls. They were seated in the same arrangement as in Agnes's house, but now they were all looking at him, with wide dark eyes.

'Well done, Louie.'

It was Zara, standing slightly to the side. She put her arms around his shoulders and gave him a hug.

Swallow sidled up to them.

'Yes, not bad for a first time. I confess I didn't think you had it in you.' She slapped him on the back.

Confused, Louie suddenly found himself back in the large room at Agnes'. The sibyls had finished their dreaming and were dispersing. Some congratulated him, while others just smiled in his direction.

'I'm not sure what I've done,' he said. 'What happened?'

'I take it back,' Swallow groaned. 'He *is* a simpleton!' She gathered up her belongings and left the room.

'It's fine, Louie. It's disorienting at first. Don't get confused, just try to retain the feeling.' Zara hugged him again, cementing the moment. 'It's best to let the experience settle in slowly.'

She suddenly gripped him tightly and kissed him on the cheek. Louie instantly felt calmer. He felt a growing warmth on his cheeks which quickly turned to heat, flushing across his face and neck. His ears felt like someone had set them alight, they burned so hot.

'That's better,' said Zara. 'That distracted you from your thoughts on the impossibility of dreaming. We'll talk again about it later, when you have absorbed the experience a little more.'

12

At the large refectory table in the dining room, Louie found himself sitting next to Zara. Most of the people he had seen in the dreaming session were settled around the table. It had been dressed with bowls of salads and fruit. There was fresh bread in baskets and various dishes which smelt heavenly.

He listened to the conversation around the table as people ate. He saw that these people were bright, and by their conversation it was apparent that they were well-informed about current issues. He thought this was surprising for sibyls — and these were surely sibyls. He picked at some of the food and watched the interactions. Zara was discussing the present limitations placed on the liminals by the government and the recent demonstrations. He was drawn out of his thoughts by a question from a tall young man seated opposite him.

'Louie, what do you think about the new restrictions being placed on the liminals?'

'Well . . . I have to be honest with you . . . until very recently I didn't have a very good opinion of the liminals. Basically, I saw them as fakes and frauds.'

Laughter erupted around the table.

'I thought their beliefs were a throwback to irrational, magical thinking.'

'Understanding is difficult without experience,' said the sibyl.

'Now that you have had a taste of our experience, how do you feel?'

'I'm not sure what you mean,' said Louie.

'I mean that we're all liminals here now!'

'Sorry?'

'Jon means that you are a liminal too, Louie,' said Zara.

'What? I'm not a fuh-fuh-f-king' liminal!'

He stood up in one movement, knocking his chair over behind him.

'I see Mr Tourette is back in the house,' Swallow offered from the other end of the table, smiling broadly.

'Ju-Ju-Just don't guh-guh-go there, Swallow,' Louie stuttered, feeling his anger rising.

Louie found himself no longer standing. Somehow, his chair had righted itself and he was sitting in front of his meal as he had been before.

He looked at Zara. She smiled.

He looked over at Swallow, but she was eating and barely returned his glance. It was as if she hadn't registered his outburst; in fact, looking round the table, it seemed like none of them had. Louie wondered if he should apologise for swearing at her, but to be fair, Swallow knew exactly how to push his buttons.

He turned to face Zara, who was still smiling at him.

'What happened?'

'We've started a different thread,' she said in a low voice. 'You've been given a chance to begin again on this topic.'

'How?'

'That's a difficult one to answer. We are faced with a fluid sense of place and time here. There's something special about this place which allows us to obtain a different standpoint . . . if we are fluid enough ourselves to grasp the moment. You obviously are, and therefore you may as well make use of it.'

'None of this makes sense, I can't grasp it, I . . .' Louie was starting to shake.

'Calm down or you'll jump again. You have to work calmly with this kind of environment; when you get worked up like this you perforate the film that binds us together and push through to another alternative situation.'

'But—'

'Stay calm Louie, let it all wash over you. It really doesn't matter that you have rational objections to the situation. They have no purchase here. The situation has you, not the reverse. You're like the cat that can't wait to be fed. You're sitting looking at the door through which the owner always brings your bowl of food; you can't see anything else. Let go of your hunger, little kitten!' Zara grinned at him.

If it was anyone but Zara who had spoken to him like that he would have exploded, but there was something about her tone which always calmed him.

'Louie, what do you think about the restrictions being placed on the liminals?' Jon was asking the question again.

Here he was again in the moment, perfectly lucid now. He decided to speak from the momentary calm space he found himself occupying. 'Liminals may have unusual abilities compared to most people, but ultimately they're humans too — they should have the same rights as anyone else.'

Jon nodded and carried on eating. Zara smiled and took some food herself. Louie was surprised at the words he had just uttered and looked around the table expecting people to remember his previous outburst, but it was as if the incident had never happened.

Later, the two of them strolled through the orchard where they had watched the light-gathering exercises a few days ago. Louie noticed that Zara was wearing an InfoWatch. Astonished, he couldn't take his eyes off it. Zara laughed at his reaction.

'Well, we're supposed to wear them as sibyls, aren't we?'

'But you're not a sibyl!' Louie answered quickly.

'Technically, I am.'

'You don't look like one.'

'So I am a different-looking one. It is true that there is a particular body type that is common among the sibyls. I think they were the early adopters, so to speak.' She smiled at her use of the terminology. 'Since then the sibyl morphology has

85

become much more diverse.'

'Are the others here all sibyls too?'

'Of course, but more developed. Upgrades, in your terminology.'

'Even Agnes?'

'Especially Agnes. She changed very early on and already had a personal history that was helpful in that change.'

'What about the men?'

'All sibyls, but they wouldn't use that term to describe themselves.'

Louie gazed at the sky. The white clouds moved fast high overhead.

'Do you want to ask the final question?'

He turned to look at her. For once, she seemed to have stored away the smile and had adopted a more solemn expression. She looked like a stone statue, her mouth no more than the faintest smirk in marble.

He swallowed then said, 'Am I a . . .?'

'Of course! Why do you think you're here?'

'B-B-But I—'

'You were given a personal message, if you remember, by the sibyl at ReachOut. You saw yourself in her role.'

'How do you know this?' Louie felt his old irritation rising.

'Don't get peevish. I saw it in my dreaming — I've been keeping an eye on you. Sometimes we find that our pet hates mean more to us than we thought. You were already a sibyl Louie, you just didn't know it.'

Louie turned around to look back towards the house, avoiding what she had said. He still couldn't make head nor tail of the buildings, except for the double doors they had just passed through that led out through the courtyard. Beyond the house was a border of trees and he could hear the movement of water in the burn that ran alongside the cottage.

'You're getting much better at taking time out, instead of just being possessed by your emotions,' Zara smiled.

He nodded. 'I am more emotional than I ever thought I was. I thought I was rational, but I see how quickly the fuse burns now.'

'Try this.'

Zara was standing in a martial arts posture, legs widely spaced, and was moving her arms slowly forward and backwards. One arm moved forward as the other moved back, but they spiralled past each other, creating a hypnotising movement.

Louie copied what she was doing. He felt stupid and a little hot, but as he concentrated on the movements, he began to relax and felt cooler. As he watched Zara's arm movements he saw the InfoWatch appearing and disappearing from under her loose cotton sleeve.

'What utilities do you have installed on it?' he asked, nodding his head towards the watch.

She stopped moving and offered him her wrist. He looked at her personal data display.

'This can't be right,' he said, puzzled. 'Zara, you currently seem to have the physiology of a thirty-four stone sumo wrestler, and you're identified as being in Tokyo right now. Your real time upload isn't correctly registering you at all!'

'It could be me,' she protested, laughing. 'I had a bit of a thing once about Japanese rice crackers and sake.'

Louie looked at her, speechless. He was learning to live with her unpredictability, but sometimes she still surprised him. He could never be sure if she was telling him the truth or some kind of story. She seemed so light, without concerns or worries. He felt himself to be the opposite; he was constantly concerned about what people thought of him, about what direction the world should be going in . . . and about the risks of irrationality and intuition. He had a sudden memory of himself standing in his bedroom here that first night, vowing to expose Zara and her friends as dangerous freaks. That moment seemed a lifetime away now.

Marsden looked up between the buildings at the darkening sky, which had become tinged with an unusual green hue. The wind had dropped and the rain, which had seemed endless for weeks now, had ceased altogether. A curious stillness — an eye of the storm, a break in the weather. A void like this meant that something was about to happen.

Marsden watched as the number of liminals in the square began to grow, the majority of them gathered around the hi-tech shop. Some went inside, others lined up by the display windows. The newest InfoWatches were on display; they boasted version 8.00 operating systems with full spectrum monitoring capacity, providing a complete control system for your personal life-environment. Everything could be controlled through the emotional and physiological reactions sensed by the InfoWatch. Switch on the TV, close your curtains, start your car, even turn the kettle on: all with hands-free operation. Advertised under the banner of Take Control of Your Life, this was the most revolutionary hardware and software launch since the beginning of the InfoWatch.

The store was already full of people queuing to buy the new watches. They had arrived early and some had queued all night. A huddle of blanketed pioneers was at the front of the queue, dreaming of God-like omnipotence while waiting for the store to open. This small party were now led into the store first and allowed to test the new equipment while photos were taken and a news crew recorded brief interviews. Just as they were about to end the interview, the camera caught sight of a number of women in dark clothing, to all appearances sibyls, edging close to the main display area.

Marsden wandered by the aisle in an act of anthropology he thought. All too quickly, one of the women swung a baseball bat at the diminutive InfoWatch on the main display. It splintered into a hundred pieces, small fragments of glass and metal flying across the room. One piece achieved short-term celebrity status by following a trajectory straight towards the video camera being used by the news team. The cameraman saw it at the last minute, as the sound of glass hitting glass rang out. He looked slightly shocked, but obviously decided that the show must go on and started filming the mayhem in the store. It seemed that there were sibyls everywhere, swinging baseball bats and iron bars, mashing up electronic equipment on every display. They worked silently amongst the crunching and splintering sounds which filled the room.

The other customers were in a state of shock. Some tried to stop the destruction but got pushed aside. Some of the more persistent ones collected a blow from the bats themselves. By the time the store security had pulled itself away from an early tea break, most of the damage had been done. The TV crew had caught all the action and the footage was soon playing everywhere, even on the few televisions left undamaged in the store. The police had arrived en masse shortly after the violence had begun, but the sibyls had seemed to just disappear, fading into the crowds of surprised shoppers. Soon, none of the dark-clothed individuals were left in the store.

Marsden was outside the shop after the violence had erupted, and he recognised one of the women talking to a policeman. He was sure she had been wielding the baseball bat against the devices only a short while ago but the policeman's manner was friendly. He walked over to them curiously. Glancing round, the woman saw Marsden's approach and edged away. He followed her and caught up with her.

'Excuse me, madam, weren't you one of the demonstrators?'

She kept walking and answered Marsden by looking back over her shoulder. 'Sorry, I'm not sure what you mean.'

'Can you stop a moment, please?'

Marsden reached and touched her shoulder lightly.

'Get off!' She turned abruptly pulling Marsden's hand away from her shoulder. 'Mind your own business, old man!' She gave him an angry look and then walked briskly away.

Marsden realised what was going on. The whole thing had been a construction, an invented drama. The women had been supposed to look like sibyls, but he suspected they were not.

The incident had dissipated quickly. To mark the occasion, the wind and rain returned. The downpour only added to the mayhem, as the police guided the remaining bystanders out of the shop across small piles of broken glass and plastic. Marsden turned from the scene and walked away.

13

The small dark figure moved quietly through the supermarket. People were casually observing her, and every now and then they checked that their watches were working properly. Contagion always begins quickly. One woman with a full shopping trolley and three vocal children in tow began to panic. She had seen that her watch was giving warnings of an impending earthquake. At the same time, the youngest of her children began to fill the trolley with his favourite chocolate biscuits.

'Put them back!' she screamed. 'We're getting out of here!'

Apocalyptic messages began appearing on most people's devices. A large man standing near the till glanced at his watch and saw a flood warning. A number of people remembered the recent warnings given by the government, which suggested that the sibyls were generating waves of misinformation in order to create panic in the population.

The sibyl in the supermarket was now being followed by a small group who were shouting at her and taunting her. She suddenly stopped walking and stood calmly facing them. Her posture was relaxed, her face serene. As the small crowd watched her, her image slowly began to fade, disappearing rapidly into thin air. Some shoppers gasped or exclaimed in astonishment, but most of them looked dazed and wandered away back to their shopping, accepting the strange event as if it was a dream.

Charlotte was sitting in a corner of the living room talking to herself and to two of her dolls.

'He's a very bad man and needs telling off.' She paused and made one of the dolls more comfortable by pushing its legs into a sitting position. 'Yes, it is true what you say,' she continued. 'We will rise up against him.'

Paul stopped writing and turned around, curious to hear such a sentence uttered by his six-year-old daughter. 'Charlotte, what were you talking about?'

'Just talking with Alison.'

'The doll?'

'Yes, Alison Fraser.' She lowered her voice as if communicating a secret. 'But Alison doesn't know she's a doll so keep it quiet.'

Paul smiled. Sometimes the things that Charlotte said tickled him. She really did have a great imagination. 'You said something about a bad man?'

'Oh nothing, just a bad man that Alison said came into her dreams.'

'Not in your dreams?'

'No, I don't know him.'

'What did the man do in Alison's dream?'

'He tried to control her. He made her wear a watch, even though she doesn't want to.'

'What did you say about rising up against him?'

'Oh Dad, it's just kid's stuff. Don't worry.'

She wore a look that was years beyond her age, that made Paul feel silly, an over-concerned parent. He turned away as he heard a news story breaking on the TV.

'The government has confirmed that from today, all certified liminals will be required by law to wear a communication device at all times. Non-compliance could incur detention in a re-education centre, or even stricter measures.'

Paul turned the volume up.

'The legislation gives the police the right to arrest and detain citizens until evidence is provided that they are not involved in terrorism. There have been a growing number of acts of terrorism since Mendesgate five years ago and the government is committed to avoiding any further events that could compromise national security. It has been suggested that most of the European Union will follow the USA and the UK and adopt this policy in due course.'

The presenter dropped his manufactured expression of concern and replaced it with a white toothy smile.

'Now, on a lighter note, the winner of "I wish I was a celebrity" has been announced and will soon be on tour! The lucky individual will also be taking part in a new soap opera . . .'

Paul switched the TV off. Behind him, Charlotte was still chastising one of her dolls.

It had to happen, Paul thought. The tensions had been growing daily with the sibyls. Only last week, there had been an early morning raid on a house in the next street which was supposed to be related to cyber-terrorism activities. As far as he knew, there had been no convictions and no one had seen any of the women who had been arrested since. The house had been left empty. It had been burgled soon after, and the graffiti sprayed on the front of the house was full of anti-liminal sentiment.

As far as he knew, the sibyls had lived there without any problems for the last year and a half. They were scapegoats, and when you thought about the issue it was only a short step to legislating that all people were required to wear a device all the time. It was already recommended that everyone should wear them for personal health and security reasons. The sibyls were an easy target for sure. Paul was certain that most of them were not involved in any subversive actions and yet they were being demonised. It had to be said that governments all over were becoming ever more controlling. The pattern was set.

Charlotte Mendes' actions had resulted in embarrassment for the intelligence agencies and the government. He supposed it was a calculated strategy by the government: blame the sibyls, make them public enemy number one — a simple distraction from what was really going on. Marsden had told him about the sibyls destroying the watches at the opening of the tech shop. From what he knew of the sibyls, it just did not seem likely at all. Marsden had told him that he thought the disturbance had been choreographed and acted out by crisis actors. Paul had never heard the term before, but Marsden assured him that they were used to ensure that the preferred interpretation of an event was communicated to the public by the media.

When he thought about it, he had to agree with Marsden. Politicians and corporate executives were all about image these days. They projected a picture, a world of their own devising. But then they promptly forgot that it was imagined and assumed it to be true. In order to maintain their world they had to manufacture events which were true to their creation. It dawned on him that he could be talking about psychotics instead of politicians. Who was it who had said that psychopaths were often at the top of every organisation?

Having built their own fantasy world, those in charge had too much to lose if their world was perceived as threatening by others. The best form of defence was to attack and if you didn't have someone threatening to attack, then by necessity you had to manufacture an enemy. Wars always appeared when there were threats to the economy and the underlying vested interests. This was the same phenomenon, just on a larger scale. He had always been sceptical about politics and big business, but seeing how Charlotte had been treated by the authorities, and latterly spending time with Marsden, had heightened his cynicism.

'You must put on your watch, PUT IT ON!'

Charlotte was acting out the bad man putting a watch on a sibyl doll. Paul watched and shook his head in disbelief. She had anticipated the story on the news. He tried not to think about the possibility that his daughter might be a sibyl. If she was, what kind of future did she face?

14

The large electric gates closed smoothly behind Deacon's Mercedes as he pulled into his driveway. The house was modern, large and completely lacking in any distinctive features that would mark it out from the others in this exclusive community. The driveway led through manicured gardens, which from a bird's eye view looked like the exact geometric representations of houses and gardens you might see in a virtual reality game or simulated world. Getting out of the car, he was met by the family dog. It ran towards him, its tail wagging furiously and emitting short excited barks. Deacon patted the dog's head and it responded by pushing lightly back against his hand.

He tapped the security code into the door lock and the door clicked open. Inside the house, the rooms and decor were as controlled and precise as the lawns outside. He put his briefcase down in the hall and put his coat and hat on the coat stand. Wooden panelling lined the tiled hallway; the overall effect was not unlike an important vicarage in the 1920s. Deacon's taste was somewhat old-fashioned. There was dark polished wood everywhere with traditional carpets and rugs, pale painted walls, heavy plum-coloured curtains capped by elaborate pelmets. Modest chandeliers hung from the ceilings in most rooms.

The place was silent as he walked through to the kitchen at the rear of the house. He could hear the strains of a radio play. As he entered the room, he was met by a pleasant smile.

'Hello dear! I did not hear you come in. I was busy making cakes.'

She smiled perfectly again. He regarded his new wife. She looked like a model in a 1950s advertisement for kitchen white goods: pinafore, A-line dress, perfectly coiffured hair and a little heavy on the make-up.

They exchanged pecks on the cheek and she quickly prepared a cup of tea for Deacon.

'There we are. Just how you like it, dear.'

She moved around the kitchen, lightly attending to an endless series of little tasks.

'How was your day, dear? Fruitful I hope?'

For a few seconds there was only the sound of the radio play in the room, a distraction only if you thought it had any merit.

'Fine.'

'Oh that is good, I am pleased.' She was still flitting between work surfaces.

Deacon emptied his cup and left the room. He entered his office and placed the briefcase on the desk. He slowly opened the locks and drew back the top to reveal a set of papers. The front page bore the title 'The Implications of the Reverse Algorithm'. It was stamped 'Top Secret'. This, he thought, would prove to be the turning point. At last, any resistance would be overcome.

Deacon firmly believed that the world needed strong leadership, an iron rod wielding authority so that everyone knew their place and understood their role. Society should be like a well-tuned and oiled machine with an expert driver. Over the years, he had practised what he preached and considered himself a strong leader. Discipline, vision and control were his watchwords. He had employed this philosophy even with his family. Spare the rod, spoil the child. He had no time for the kind of modern parenting which presumed that you should not spank the child. His children had always been polite, well-behaved and courteous and had grown up into responsible adults. He trusted this was because of his parenting style. People used to comment on how obedient the children were when they were young —

proof that his particular blend of discipline was successful.

The fact that he had not seen the children in years was, he believed, due to their own shortcomings. Their mother had left him years ago. No note, no inkling it was going to happen and no contact since then. But what really hurt him was the loss of his only daughter. She was so unlike him . . . she was dreamy, imaginative and intuitive, but he had pulled her back to the rational world time and time again. He remembered the bullying she had suffered at school. He had tried to tell her she would not be successful unless she became tougher and stood up for herself. But it hadn't worked. She was different, he knew that, and so he had endeavoured to help her build up the characteristics that she would need to be successful in life: how to handle people, how to use opportunities to climb the social ladder and keep those below you in order. He thought he had been successful, but she had left anyway. She was only fifteen when she had disappeared. Not long afterwards, distraught over the girl's disappearance, his wife had gone, taking their son with her. He had employed a private detective to find them, but no traces of any of them had been uncovered. It had been ten years now. Deacon had kept all their rooms the same, just as they had left them. He continued to wait for news, but it never came.

Three years ago, he had decided that he ought to take advantage of the developments in robotics and prosthetic science. He bought a simulant dog which brought some life back to the house. He updated its behavioural repertoire a year later, which had given him the incentive to try other simulants. He had bought the synthetic that was in the kitchen now, which had been marketed under the name Martha. She had not filled the gap. Deacon believed devoutly in a mechanistic future; after all, humans were just biological machines. But somehow the simulant lacked something. Perhaps it could be remedied in a future update, but at the moment she fell short of his expectations. He filled the gap with work and had managed to rise to the most senior position in his department. In a way, he was now the head of a much larger family. Society itself relied on him. And Deacon was determined to keep it safe from the dangers of irrationality by controlling the ever-growing flood of liminals.

'I must admit, I'm a little nervous about visiting a group like this.'

Paul glanced briefly at Marsden, who was checking the road map. They left the junction and headed for the motorway.

'Well, it will be good to see an active group of sibyls who are prepared to talk about their experiences,' Marsden said, returning his gaze to the map.

'There's one thing I don't understand. Why would the government fund your project?'

'Our project,' Marsden corrected him.

'Okay, why would the government fund our project just as they decide to legislate that sibyls should be monitored permanently? It doesn't add up.'

Paul accelerated and started to overtake a large truck making slow progress on the outer lane.

'My boy, I'm amazed that you've reached your age without realising the duplicitousness of politicians. It is always a Hegelian dialectic: government has to keep all voters onside to preserve their own situation. Some people want rid of the sibyls, others are sympathetic to their plight. Big business wants better data, partly because some groups of sibyls are distorting it deliberately. The corporations would like to get rid of the sibyls but they still use them for synthesis of the data capture. So the government simultaneously employs both the carrot and the stick, making out that they're acting with both groups' interests in mind. They try to keep everyone happy. Of course, it's not about actually doing something but being seen to be doing something, which is infinitely more important to them. Having said that, I do think there are elements in government who are on something of a witch-hunt. Another world view is being born and the stalwarts of the old paradigm don't like it and don't want it.'

'What do you mean, the old paradigm?' Paul asked.

'Philosophy of science. The historian Thomas Kuhn said that

ideas are held and expressed by communities of scientists. New ideas appear when the models held by the incumbent authorities can no longer adequately explain anomalous phenomena. Sibyls are just such an anomaly; our current sages don't know what to do with this anomaly and prefer to see it as fakery and fraud. New ideas may have a chance of explaining the phenomena, but they have no credibility while the old timers still control the system or paradigm. New paradigms can only get a grip when the old paradigmers die out.'

'If I understand you correctly, that really puts pressure on the typical view of science as being a journey towards having a complete picture of the world.'

'Exactly. Kuhn was horsewhipped for this theorem and had to dilute some of his ideas, otherwise the club wouldn't talk to him again.'

'The club?'

'Other academics, scientists, philosophers, et cetera.'

'Really?'

'Sure. Academia and science is very much a club; if you step out of line or discuss things which are considered beyond the pale, you're seen as a maverick, an unreliable person — you get cut off! I've experienced it first-hand.'

'So, how do you feel about these visitors who are arriving shortly?'

Zara was helping Agnes dry the dishes in the kitchen.

'Well . . . it's an interesting development, but I suspect it won't really help us. I'm intrigued that they have chosen to frame their investigation of us as research, rather than intervention. Marsden is actually an interesting character. When I spoke to him, he was very sympathetic and his story rang true to me. I'm only letting them visit us because he's involved. Anyway, the government security official threatened us with a fine if we didn't cooperate with these visits.'

'How did they know there might be sibyls here?'

Agnes shrugged. 'Perhaps it's something to do with dodgy data being returned from com devices . . .?'

She turned to Zara and gave her a quizzical look.

'I can't imagine who would do that,' Zara said, smiling innocently.

'We'll see what happens when they arrive. Tell the others to hold off on anything too outrageous until we gauge what they're like in person.'

'Will do.'

Zara caught sight of Louie descending the stairs. 'Louie . . . looking good.'

Louie had shaved off his beard.

'Er, hi.' He rubbed his chin self-consciously as he entered the kitchen. 'I guess I just felt like a change.'

Zara grinned at him. 'You're getting the hang of this.'

15

Paul and Marsden pulled into the Ebor car park and trawled for a space. The rain was hammering down. Marsden had been here before; whenever he travelled to Scotland he always chose to stop off and eat at Ebor. Motorway cafes in Britain were notorious for overpriced, low nutrition cellophane-wrapped snacks warmed up in microwaves by sullen teenagers. The corporate world had spent years turning food into packaged abstractions which promised a lot but delivered very little. Ebor was a refreshing change — real cooked food served by people who knew how to handle a cooker. It had been started by a farming family who were obviously still rooted in reality.

They strolled between the food counters looking at what was on offer. There were already quite a few customers looking to fill up, even though it was only just midday. Marsden chose some rustic steak pie with potatoes and vegetables. Pleasantly surprised at the range of meals on offer, Paul settled for lasagna. Silence descended onto their table by the window as they tucked into the food. After a while, Marsden posed a question.

'What was Charlotte Mendes like?'

'In what way?'

'Just your impressions.'

'When I first met her she was in a really bad way, almost catatonic . . . she could barely speak. She had been overmedicated and I realise now that it was to keep her silent. The Mindwire project was devised by Sandesman, the head psychiatrist at the hospital, and his colleagues. They decided to hide the casualties of the project behind permanent psychiatric conditions. As Charlotte came off the drugs, we realised there were no problems other than those she had suffered as a consequence of the treatment and detainment. She was bright and able.'

'What kinds of abilities did she have?'

'I didn't think there was anything unusual at first but it became apparent that she had a high level of intuition. She could correctly guess long sequences of ESP Zener cards in tests. You know these types of cards?'

'Yes.'

'Well, she could predict a whole pack, not getting a single one wrong. She also made specific predictions about people. There was one incident when she was still in hospital, she suggested that one of my clients had died. Sadie and I checked it out. We found him not dead but sleeping in a coffin in his living room.'

Marsden looked puzzled.

'Yes, I know, a little strange, but Eldred was always a bit unusual. So Charlotte saw something that was quite like the actual event but not fully accurate . . . interpretation must have played a part.'

'I understand from the research literature that extrasensory perception is not like perception at all; it seems to be more like the process that underlies memory,' said Marsden. 'We sense things through a web of emotional nuances and resonances very much like the process of dreaming. Dreams are composed of our feelings about things happening in our lives, enabling us to make sense of them in relation to our level of development.'

'Like Jung's idea of compensation?'

'Yes. We learn about ourselves in dreams . . . the aspects we are not conscious of eventually become more prominent as a consequence. A good idea, I always thought. It's a shame that dreams are just seen as the visible machinations storing up memories these days.'

'The dreams of the sibyls seem to be quite a different phenomenon,' said Paul.

Marsden nodded. 'Mmm. From what I understand, the sibyls are able to generate dreams on demand and use them to include others. More startling perhaps are their claims that their dreams are becoming real. Have you seen your client recently who was having those sorts of experiences?'

'Yes, Carla you mean? I saw her last week. She's still convinced that's what's happening.'

Marsden drained his teacup. 'You know, I keep being reminded of the Australian aborigines who see their Dreaming as creating the world. Quite apt really — if the sibyls actually are creating real-life situations through their dreaming. Fascinating.'

'It'll be interesting to see what this visit brings, what these sibyls can do.'

'Well, we'd better make a move if we're going to get there before it goes dark. You enjoyed the food?'

'Yes. I wouldn't have believed that real food still existed in motorway cafes like this.'

After another two hours of featureless motorway, they followed a B road that turned into a maze of small country lanes. Thick hedgerows loomed either side of the narrow roads as they drove through the dusk. Paul turned off the road onto the lane which led to the centre. The land was mostly heath and rock with occasional stands of pine trees.

'Obviously an old drover's road,' Marsden observed, folding away the map.

'Why do you say that?'

'The stand of Scots pine trees we just passed. They usually signify an old collection point where the drovers would rest.'

'Hmm.' Paul's eyes were growing tired. He hoped it wouldn't be too long before they arrived at this place; it was certainly out of the way.

'There you go: confirmation!'

Marsden celebrated by throwing the map over his head into the back seat. They were passing a pub, aptly named 'The Drovers'.

103

'Take the next right,' Marsden directed. 'The track may look a little rough, but it should take us to the sibyls' centre.'

They followed the track, which was overhung by trees, their bare winter branches moving in a gentle breeze. The overhang created a living tunnel which made it impossible to see much of the landscape either side of the road. Eventually, the tunnel opened out into a large space sheltered by a tall brick wall. They parked next to an old Land Rover. As if out of nowhere, a small reception party appeared.

As they got out of the car two women approached, a young blond-haired girl with a distinctive smile wearing an indigo dress and an older Chinese woman, who Paul judged to be older than she looked. They shook hands and exchanged names. Agnes inquired politely as to their journey and invited them into the house.

'It has been a long journey for you both. Have you eaten?'

'We did, but a while ago now,' said Marsden.

'I have some soup and freshly made bread ready. Please make yourselves comfortable and I'll fetch it for you.' Agnes disappeared into the kitchen. Zara stood calmly by the dresser and regarded them, smiling.

'You're very kind,' Marsden shouted after Agnes.

A sense of complete peace seemed to envelope the old farmhouse. Feeling a little uncomfortable, Paul broke the silence.

'How long have you been here, Zara?'

'Oh, it must be five years or more, but I'm not sure. Time seems elastic around here.'

Before Paul could ask what she meant, Agnes returned and ushered them to a sturdy oak dining table on which she had placed bowls of hot soup and some fragrant bread.

'Here we are then. While you're eating, we'll sort out your rooms and carry up your luggage for you.'

'The soup smells heavenly,' said Marsden appreciatively.

'You made the bread too?' Paul turned and looked at Agnes but it was Zara who answered.

'Yes. Agnes is a treasure, she keeps us all well fed and cared for.'

Zara put her arm around Agnes' shoulder and the older woman smiled.

'We try to be as self-sufficient as we can with fruit and vegetables but we buy in the flour. It's a good life here,' she added. She turned to Zara. 'Let's leave them to eat in peace. Just shout if you need anything, there's always someone around.'

'They're certainly very hospitable.' Paul spooned some soup into his mouth.

'Mmmm, wonderful soup,' enthused Marsden. 'I spent some time in China doing research; this is the old way. The poorest people will offer you tea if that is all they have and whenever possible they will try to provide a feast. Food is central to the Chinese character. Do you know that the phrase "Have you eaten?" was a common form of greeting during the hard times under Mao.'

Paul picked up some of the bread. It was like the bread he remembered from childhood, which even then had been in short supply as the ubiquitous industrially manufactured white sliced came to dominate the market. The outside crust was crispy like that of a French baguette, but the shape was round and squat.

'I know what you're thinking,' Marsden piped up. 'Why does it taste so different? And why don't people make their own bread anymore?'

'I think people assume they can't do it or have no time to do it,' mused Paul.

'How are we doing?' Agnes entered the room. 'Your things are in your rooms; when you've finished I'll show you around. Was the food all right?'

'Thanks, it was delicious Agnes.' Marsden smacked his lips with satisfaction.

'Good, I am pleased. I am from a Chinese family and the old ways stay with me even here in Scotland. It is important to receive guests properly, and energetically it means that you take in some of the energy of this place and begin to understand it too. It is a way of understanding us with the body, not just with the mind. Do you know what I mean?'

Marsden sneaked a quick look at Paul, wondering if he realised that they were already gathering information.

They followed Agnes out of the small dining room into a corridor from which there seemed to be multiple exits and entrances. Two doors down, they turned into another corridor where their bedrooms were located. The rooms were small, almost like monastery cells. Each one contained only a simple bed, a wooden chair and a small cupboard. Their bags were on the beds.

'If you need anything, just say.'

'Thank you, Agnes, you are very kind,' Paul said.

'We're shortly about to start evening dreaming practice, so if you want to see that feel free to come along. We will be in the large dining room at the end of this corridor.'

'We're certainly very interested, and will see you shortly.'

Marsden bowed his head slightly as he spoke. Agnes returned the gesture ever so subtly and left them. Before returning to his room Marsden turned to Paul. 'Interesting, don't you think? And it's still only the first evening. It will be good to see what kind of setup they have here.'

'I agree. They seem very open to sharing their experiences. I think I'll quickly unpack before we head to the practice room.'

Paul emptied a few clothes into the little bedside cupboard and put his bag under the bed. As he did so, a large striped cat appeared in the doorway. It looked Paul directly in the eye, narrowed its eyes in a cat kiss and padded silently out the door.

Marsden looked up as the cat sauntered into his room. 'Hullo!'

The cat sat upright on a patterned rug, looked at Marsden and then walked slowly out into the corridor. Marsden followed it, but by the time he peered around the door the cat had already disappeared. He returned to his room and laid out his clothes, putting his phone and a couple of books onto the small bedside table.

16

Paul and Marsden managed to find their way to the large dining room but not without a couple of diversions. The house's floor plan was indeterminable. Numerous small rooms branched off long narrow corridors, creating the sense of a maze or labyrinth. As they wended their way down the corridors, the house was almost silent and Marsden wondered whether or not anyone else was there. But when they reached the dining room they saw at least twenty people standing about and chatting in small groups. The group was mainly composed of women, with just a few men among them. About half of the women looked like sibyls; they were small, dark haired, brown eyed and most were wearing loose clothes. It reminded Marsden of a 1960s ashram, except there was no central yogic figure to which all attention was directed.

Agnes made some brief introductions, introducing Marsden and Paul as scientists employed on a government project to study the sibyls' abilities. From their expressions, Paul got the impression that the group had already been appraised of the situation.

Marsden thanked her and then said, 'We're very pleased to be here and grateful for the opportunity to have a glimpse into your lives and practices. We would like to assure you that we are not here to interfere or criticise your way of living. We just want to observe. My colleague, Dr Paul Clark, is a psychologist and I'm an anthropologist, so we'll be trying to understand what you do through the methods of these disciplines.'

Agnes inclined her head in his direction.

'Thank you, Dr Marsden. If everybody takes their place perhaps we can show our visitors the basics of dreaming.'

The group took their places, seated cross-legged on the floor in a large circle. They rested their hands lightly on their knees and dipped their heads slightly as if leaning forward. To the untrained observer nothing much seemed to be happening, but both Paul and Marsden sensed how the group radiated an undivided sense of purpose, a kind of subtle coherence.

Agnes, Zara and the others sensed the energetics of each other quickly, and combined their thoughts. Group dreaming like this was powerful. It was easier to attain the beginnings of the dreaming state in a group, but it could be hard to keep on track if someone shifted their attention at a different time to the others.

In her mind's eye, Zara saw a pulsing light at the centre of the group. She knew that this was the combined attention of the dreamers. When it gained enough intensity it would spread to envelop the room.

Marsden watched silently. He looked at the faces of the dreamers, eyes partly closed and facing the floor. He could see no movement in any of the participants, not even a tiny muscle tremor.

Watching carefully, Paul thought he sensed a sudden change in the light in the room. He couldn't be sure, but it felt like sunlight had come in from outside. Puzzled, he looked around for the source of the illumination. He couldn't see any windows in this room and, anyway, it was night-time. It happened again, like a small flash of light in the centre of the circle. Paul glanced at Marsden, whose expression seemed to say 'Stay calm'. Paul could feel his heart beating faster than usual and returned his gaze to the centre of the circle. The light flashed again; it seemed to be becoming more frequent.

Zara felt the pulse deep inside her. They had generated enough energy between them and coherence was peaking. It was now time to release the collected energy and see where it took them.

Marsden didn't have time to blink. The room, the circle of people, even Paul who had been sitting next to him, were gone. He was standing alone on a sandy beach. The colour of the sky was a blueish green, suggesting that a storm was coming. He looked inland at the vegetation; the lush greenery hinted at a tropical location. There was no sign of habitation anywhere. The land climbed quickly from sea level, forming small hills studded with outcrops of rock. Wherever he was, the day was nearing its end — he could see the crescent of the moon just over the bluff of the cliff at the far end of the beach. He turned to face the sea. He held his breath and spun round to look again at the moon over the cliff. There were two moons! How could that be?

He saw two figures approaching from further down the beach. He recognised the young blond woman as Zara, and she was with Paul. He walked towards them, shouting a greeting. They waved and soon closed the distance.

'Dr Marsden,' said Zara with a laugh in her voice. 'You went a little astray. We intended for you both to stay together — at least on this first attempt. The experience can be a little confusing otherwise.'

'Marsden, can you believe this?'

Paul was visibly excited. He knelt down and grasped a handful of sand and, amazed, watched it fall in clumps from his hand. He ran to the water's edge and washed his hand, marvelling at the drops of water running down his arm.

'Zara, how stable is this view?' Marsden asked.

'It will stay as long as we intend it to, assuming there are no unusual atmospheric or environmental conditions.'

At the water's edge, Paul was picking up one pebble after another. The pebbles were clear, like glass, but they had warmth and texture. He lifted one above his head, looking through it at the sky.

Marsden turned to Zara again. 'And where are we?'

'Another world.'

'Literally?'

Zara laughed. 'Yes. This is a world we found in our dreams. We use it to measure our development. It takes a very finely tuned dreaming ability to reach this place. Agnes said we should show you some basic dreaming, but I thought what the hell, we should take you to the outer limits. Time is short anyway.'

'Why is time short?'

Marsden thought she looked preoccupied.

'The commune . . . I've seen things in my dreams—' Suddenly she stopped herself. 'Look, we have to leave now. Dr Clark, are you ready to return?'

Paul stuffed a glass pebble into his pocket and rejoined Marsden and Zara.

There was a flash of greenish light and when Marsden's eyes refocused he was back in the large room with the others. The dreamers were still sitting in their circle but shortly they began to slowly stretch and move, opening their eyes. A gentle murmur of conversation began to fill the room. As they slowly got to their feet, Marsden and Paul exchanged glances. It had been an impressive first demonstration of sibyl dreaming.

The day started early. It seemed that those practising dreaming needed less sleep than normal individuals. Paul and Marsden sat in on the 6:00 a.m. meditation session and then took breakfast with the group. They managed informal chats with most of the participants and recorded some of their discussions. At Marsden's suggestion, they made arrangements for short formal interviews with some of the participants for later during the day. At eleven, there was another group dreaming session which they were invited to attend. After their experience the day before, they both had high expectations and they were not disappointed.

Zara led the session and described in advance what they were going to do before entering the dreaming state. The proposal was to show Paul and Marsden how dreaming could connect distant sibyls.

The dreaming began in the same quiet manner as the day before. The dreamers sat in a circle, heads bowed slightly. Soon, Paul noticed slight changes in light levels and then a slow pulsing like they had observed yesterday. But this time he settled into the phenomenon and decided to try to respond less physically, and more with his mind's eye.

Across the room, he could see Marsden gazing around. Suddenly, everything changed. The room had gone, and to Paul it seemed like his awareness was not located anywhere definite, it was just hanging in darkness. There seemed to be points of light around him, some brighter, some less bright. He wasn't sure if it was that some of the lights were nearer and others further away — he had no sense of depth in this darkness and couldn't reach a decision.

One of the lights seemed to move closer to them. As Paul watched it, the point of light expanded and suddenly engulfed them. They found themselves looking out onto a rural scene, but the flora and the landscape were unexpected. Cacti, sand and rock made up much of the immediate surroundings. Nearby, there was a large round clearing in the vegetation. A group of people were sitting cross-legged in a circle, heads bowed. By their looks and dress, Paul guessed that they were Native Americans, and that they were dreaming.

Marsden wondered what the dreamers could see. Could they see the room he was in as clearly as he could see their surroundings? For a second there was a flickering between the two locations as his thought was absorbed by the dream. He heard Zara's voice.

'We have to be careful with our thoughts and not stray too far from our purpose. The energy that binds the communal dream can respond very quickly to stray thoughts. What we are seeing is another dreaming group like ours who are currently exploring as we are. This is a simple joining up of dreams with two sets of dreamers. Next, we will join a reality-making dream. Please stay calm and collected during this.'

Marsden watched the desert scene evaporate. They found themselves again in a dark space, filled with innumerable points of light, like a black starry sky. A point of light suddenly rushed towards them at speed and then they were adjusting to a new, surprising scene.

Schulz's hands twisted against the restraint of the ropes. He shook his head but couldn't remove the hood. He crouched, trembling uncontrollably. He couldn't hear anything; somehow his ears were blocked. He could sense others in the room but had no idea who they were or why they were holding him.

He knew that this was a classic terrorist holding ploy, deliberately psychologically stressful for the detainee, restrained and with limited perception. He knew all about these kinds of techniques; he had been involved in direct interrogation and debriefing earlier in his career. He remembered being put in this setting as a trainee, but it had been twenty years since that experience. Something told him that this was no training session. He couldn't think what he had done to now be on the receiving end of this kind of treatment.

Someone was near him now and tugging at the cord holding the hood in place. The hood came off but his eyes were dazzled by two bright lights pointing at him. When his vision adjusted, he could see that the walls of the room were in rough brick, squared off a dirt floor. He could just make out some other figures crouching around the perimeter of the room; they too were all bound and hooded. His attention was brought back to two figures standing in front of him. They were silhouetted against the bright light and he couldn't make out their features.

'Who are you? What do you want?'

The figures stood passively watching.

'Who are you? What do you want?'

His own words floated back to him like an echo, but it was not his voice. He could see a huddled figure against the wall to his right. The suit he was wearing, a distinctive Savile Row cloth, looked like Frobisher's.

'Frobisher, are you alright?'

There was no answer. From Frobisher's huddled posture, Schulz could tell that he hadn't even heard him. Schulz closed his eyes in despair. He had the worst kind of feelings circling in his mind.

Watching the scene, Marsden found that he could feel the emotions of the captives and even hear their thoughts. He tried to stay calm and quieten his feelings of astonishment so as not to disturb the dream. He needed to keep his questions until later.

Soon they were back in the darkness, pinpricks of light surrounding them. Zara announced that the next dream would be the last dream for that morning. Apparently, it was to be a demonstration of how the sibyls' dreaming could be used to gather information.

Now the darkness took on form, but it took Paul and Marsden a few moments to make sense of the scene. The room they were now seeing was dark, illuminated only by small strips and points of light. A large metallic framework shaped like a sphere was in the centre of the room, reflecting what little light pierced the gloom. In the centre of the sphere was a human form wearing a helmet and a skin-tight suit. Issuing from the suit was a mass of wires and electronic connections.

Inhabiting the suit was a sibyl, monitoring the information flow on ConWeb. With a jolt, Paul remembered the scene from the day Charlotte had died — the sphere, the suit, the bank of wrap-around plasma screens that he had seen on that fateful day. It seemed that in spite of public distrust and corporate denial, the sibyls were still employed to filter data.

All was quiet at first, but then, with the sound of servomotors, the metallic orb turned as if to face them. The sibyl had sensed them, and had decided to speak directly to them. The screens around the sphere all simultaneously switched to show the circle of dreamers sitting in Agnes' dining room.

A female voice spoke.

'You are welcome, friends. We are always your willing servants.'

The reply sounded like Zara. 'We thank you and your sisters; we connect in friendship and in service. We hope that we can help each other and the people when the time comes.'

'Acknowledged, friends.'

The sibyl signed off with a rapid series of connections with other sibyls worldwide. Images flashed on the screens of groups and individuals from all corners of the earth, a grand network of dreaming.

PART THREE

DELIVERANCE

17

'This is great!'

Frobisher was more excited than Schulz had ever seen him. Frobisher sat at his desk, fingers rapping nervously against the plastic oak veneer. He stood up again, grasping the memo he had just received, which was already somewhat dog-eared from the constant handling it had received.

'What is it?' Schulz asked.

Frobisher walked to the window, his leather shoes squeaking as he turned to face Schulz.

'It's great, that's what it is. Simply great. Deacon has okayed the use of the reverse algorithm.'

'What?'

'He's finally done it. Decided on a wide-scale implementation of the RA.'

Schulz couldn't hide his surprise. 'Even I didn't think he was that crazy.'

'Crazy? It's a beautiful move, it gives us complete control over the lims — and everyone else actually.'

Frobisher's reaction was over the top, Schulz thought. He reminded Schulz of those icons of the saints of the Middle Ages, clutching sacred relics and lost in some kind of divine bliss. Frobisher's eyes were cast heavenwards, his mind lost in imagining the implications of Deacon's latest decree.

Standing up, Schulz reached for the memo. 'Let me have a look. What kinds of limitations does it have on it?'

Frobisher clutched the piece of paper closer to his chest and looked alarmed. Schulz wondered if Frobisher was losing it completely.

'I just want to look at it. What's your problem?' said Schulz.

'Okay, here.' Frobisher reluctantly passed it over.

Schulz unfurled the creased little note. 'I'm just amazed that he's finally taken the leap. I didn't think he had it in him.' Schulz scanned the memo. 'Right, let's see. It says that the technique known as the reverse algorithm will be used in future events where there are serious threats to the government or the country. It will be used to disable potential terrorists and to enable security forces to enforce an arrest. It will also be used in situations where there is a high likelihood of public disruption and . . . what's this last bit? Individuals will be targeted if they have a history of cyber attacks.'

'See what I mean; beautiful.'

'But it says that it will only be employed in instances of severe impending threat,' pointed out Schulz.

Frobisher burst out laughing. 'But, but, but. No problem! Almost any situation could be argued to be a severe threat. Have you seen the latest shooting targets the police have been given? Children holding guns, pregnant women with push chairs with suspected IEDs in them. You could probably turn the reverse algorithm on a kid standing at the ice cream van taking hold of a cornet. Everyone's the enemy now, Schulz. As for the section on cyber attacks, well, that pretty much covers everything. The problem with false data transmission could be interpreted as a cyber attack.'

'That wouldn't be an attack,' protested Schulz.

'The definition of a cyber attack in the appendix of the complete document would allow it.'

Schulz shook his head. 'I think this is going to bring trouble.'

'Bring it on — we thrive on disasters! Only strife moves us forward. Anyway, what's with you? Suddenly the people's advocate or what? I thought you were serious about governing society.'

'I think those who are challenging our way of life should be disciplined and controlled, but we're all in this together. We wear the watches too. I for one don't want to be turned into a robotic zombie by the reverse algorithm. You know as well as I do that fifty per cent of our responses to terrorism are without real cause. You or I could easily be targeted; the programs aren't very accurate. They're even more inaccurate than the weather forecasts, for God's sake, and that's not saying much.'

'Well, as our computers get bigger and faster we'll nail it,' said Frobisher.

'That's what the meteorologists have been saying for decades!'

'Anyway, it's not true that we're likely to be targeted.'

'Why?'

'Grades twenty and above have anonymised status watches and devices,' said Frobisher smugly.

'What?'

'Yup. Anonymous and full indemnity.'

'I didn't know that.'

'They only tell you at grade twenty. Reach the grade, and they turn on your anonymity at the DIA. Lower grades just have to face up to the fact that everything is recorded . . . and now of course the reverse algorithm can reach them.' He saw Schulz's expression. 'Don't you think this was inevitable? The higher up the ladder you are, the more indemnity you need. We're here to manage the hordes. Sometimes, these high-level decisions are difficult and we need some insurance that the actions we take — for the benefit of all — are not misinterpreted by the simple-minded do-gooders. It's evolution; the higher up the chain you are . . .' He turned slowly to face Schulz. 'What grade are you anyway, Schulz?' he said with a sly grin.

'Eighteen,' Schulz said quietly.

'Sorry, didn't quite catch what you said?'

'I said I am a grade eighteen!' Schulz said loudly.

'Oh, that is unfortunate, Schulz.' Frobisher grinned. 'You'd better behave until you rise a couple of grades and get your anonymity.'

'The worst thing is, you wouldn't even know that you were changing behaviour.' Schulz was becoming pensive.

'Mmmm,' agreed Frobisher. 'I'm told that it creeps up on you like a gradual cold. You don't connect the small things to what's happening, just like you don't realise that your temperature has increased with the beginnings of a cold. People might sense something is happening but the change can be so gradual that it's dismissed. By that time of course, the reverse algorithm has full hold and the computers at the DIA can dictate everything you do. Change your personality, turn you into an axe murderer or even just produce a profound catalepsy. Beautiful. The ultimate in customised control of the individual. The technology has come so far now that you could create a whole new world through the algorithm and the feedback system of the InfoWatches. The individual wouldn't know what was real or completely manufactured by the central computers.'

Frobisher felt warm inside, secure in his anonymity and indemnity. Mulling it over further, he thought, they haven't a clue what's coming for them . . .

'I am frankly amazed at what you can do.' Marsden was beaming and shaking hands with each of the dreamers. 'I understand the contact with other dreams and the corporate sibyl, but what was happening in the hostage dream?'

'We wanted to show you what we call a reality dream,' said Zara. 'These are dreams that have a possibility of coming into being because of the participants' own psychological drives. The figures you saw were real people with a need for rebalancing in their life. The psyche tries to compensate for extreme behaviour. The people we saw are obviously too aggressive and controlling, so the compensatory processes set up a need for an equally controlling dream situation. Their own psyches provide the seed, or theme if you like, and we provide the dreaming energy to make it real.'

'I understand the psychological process of compensation, but in what sense is the dream real?' Paul asked.

'This is a difficult question because real is what we accept as real — what our culture accepts and what our education prepares us for. A simple explanation would be that often we just take the strength, or impact, of the event on our senses as an indication of its reality. The dreaming energy provides this strength and so makes it real.'

'I still don't get it.' Paul looked at Marsden.

'The problem is,' explained Marsden, 'that being a psychologist — a scientist — you don't have the exposure to the kinds of relativism that allows Zara's point to have any weight in the argument. You need to be more anthropological. Do you remember Jung's conversation with his assistant, Marie-Louise von Franz, about the patient who dreamed of being on the moon? Jung vehemently argued that the woman actually had been to the moon. From her rational position, von Franz argued that it wasn't possible, insisting that it was only a dream. Jung was pointing to a psychological reality which he insisted was as real as physical reality.'

'Yes, I do remember that, but the idea still seems very fuzzy to me.' Paul glanced at Zara.

'That's reality for you,' she said. 'Those things that seem simple and easy to grasp are often the most complicated when you try to delve into their true nature.'

She beamed a smile back at Paul.

'We're getting patterns which indicate a big gathering. It must be the demonstration we've been waiting for. Probabilities of it happening are twenty per cent in Trafalgar Square, thirty-seven per cent in Downing Street, seventy-three per cent and trending up for St Paul's. About 60,000 sibyls in total.'

'Are there that many sibyls?'

'Experts estimate that about one in ten humans are now sibylline.'

'How good is the information?'

'Pure blue, the highest credibility. It's based on information filtered through our sibyls. This has been trending for weeks; now it looks imminent.'

The operatives at the DIA looked at each other anxiously.

They had been preparing for months for this kind of eventuality, but nonetheless the signs and omens were unwelcome. They were not relishing the task of passing this information on to those higher up the chain.

18

Deacon had paid personal attention to the latest report on database anomalies. He paced to and fro across his office, turning sharply on his heels as he reached the boundaries of the window wall. The operatives had managed to locate the disruptive influence and Deacon was surprised and a little disconcerted at the information they had sent. Apparently, the disturbance was based in Scotland. The pattern of behaviour seemed strangely familiar and Deacon issued an immediate investigative order.

He had also put in motion another dictate which required the intelligence sibyls to have chip implants. The sibyl working in the orb at the DIA was one of the first to be implanted. She was an experiment. Data gathering would no longer be dependent on wearing the com devices, but would be trawled directly from nervous systems. If the implants could be rolled out across the population how much cleaner the data-gathering process would be. There would be no chance of terrorist sibyls faking data and creating false scenarios like those seen lately. Deacon knew that there would be some resistance — human rights and so on — but eventually the idea would embed in mass consciousness and would be seen as the norm. Direct implantation would give them the advantage of more control of the data coming in . . . and also a greater use of the reverse algorithm.

In the control room, two operators were engrossed in the display on their com devices. It was the latest craze, an immersive game using fictional themes based on real-life data supplied by the com devices.

They were paying little attention to the sibyl in the orb, who was tracking and sorting data from a signal in Scotland. The feedback had been contradictory, the data questionable. She had overridden a request to use the reverse algorithm. There was a mismatch between the individual who had been targeted and the data from her com device. Besides, to the sibyl, this individual was familiar through communal dreaming. She was a sister.

The silence at the cottage was incredible, a pure bible-black night and a silence almost palpable. An owl called, a peculiar searching screech. A bright moon cast long shadows onto the deserted garden. The sound of a twig cracking underfoot broke the silence. Then, as if out of nowhere, a crushing and splintering sound as the front door came off its hinges.

The power to the house had been cut and the bright flashlights that poured through the doorway were blinding. Chaos followed in their wake. Furniture was thrown aside, glass smashed and the sound of heavy boots storming through the house was terrifying. It seemed an eternity before the lights came back on. Army uniformed figures in riot gear filled the dining room, restraining any sibyls that tried to resist them.

'This is the one.' The uniform spoke gruffly. 'We have a ninety-eight per cent match.'

The soldier was holding Zara by the scruff of her neck. She twisted and struggled in his grasp, shouting abuse. The soldier pulled back on her neck, choking her. His superior stepped forward and barked a short order. He took hold of Zara, dragged her to her feet and pulled her towards the door.

Agnes tried to wriggle out of the grasp of the man holding her. 'What the hell are you doing? Leave her alone!'

Two soldiers moved forward and trained their firearms on Agnes, who reluctantly backed off.

Marsden could feel himself slowly recovering from the shock.

He struggled to stay calm, and addressed the nearest soldier. He could feel his blood pressure rising. 'What do you think you're doing? You have no right to do this.'

As if responding to Marsden's cue, Louie and two other men tried to break free of the grasp of their captors. Three more soldiers moved forward, guns pointing at the men.

'I want to know what you're doing? We have a right to know why we're being arrested.' Marsden spat the words out.

The soldier standing next to Marsden pushed down on his shoulder with his gun butt.

'Shut up!'

Marsden had no alternative but to kneel down again, cursing under his breath.

Zara had become silent now, even as they dragged her towards the door. She looked surprisingly composed. Calmly, she said, 'I'll be alright. Don't worry. It was inevitable.'

The soldier holding her tugged at her neck again, shutting her up as if controlling a badly behaved dog.

At a small hand signal from the superior officer, the soldiers backed out of the door, still pointing their guns at the group. Zara was dragged backwards through the door. In moments, they were gone.

'I can't believe this!' Agnes shook her head as she surveyed the room and the splintered door. She suddenly looked tired and drawn. 'Where have they taken her?' she said almost to herself.

Marsden took her by the shoulders. Her head fell forward and tears ran down her cheeks.

Marsden said, 'We'll find her, and find out what's going on. Don't worry.'

Agnes sighed and picked up an overturned chair. 'Zara has had it coming for years.'

'What do you mean?' Paul asked.

'Playing with their computers, giving the system false information . . . and dreams.'

'Dreams?'

'Yes, she's been giving the computers dreams. Lacing their

databases with dream matter, constructing a dream world. She said that she had found a way of moving through their machines as if walking through a forest path. This is obviously why they have taken her. They've found out what she's been doing.'

'How can computers dream?' Louie had been silent until now and still looked shocked.

'I think the important thing now is to get back to London to see how we can help Zara,' Marsden said.

Paul nodded, and began to head to his room to collect his belongings.

'I'll come with you,' Louie announced. 'I need to find her.'

19

The sibyl in the orb sensed that the operation was complete and mentally sent a message back to the control room. She felt guilty but she knew she had no choice. Her sister's destiny had to be fulfilled if the sibyls were to be free. The message was intercepted and forwarded to Deacon, who responded by issuing an order for an immediate implant. It was probably the only way of controlling this particular terrorist.

Zara had lost all track of time and place. They had been travelling for what seemed like hours. At the back of the army transport truck where she was being held there were no windows, so she had no idea if it was night or day. There were three soldiers guarding her, and a quick glance around the small space told her there was no chance of escape just now.

She rested her chin on her chest and tried to meditate. She was just achieving a still, calm state when the truck lurched to a stop. She waited, suddenly alert. If they were going to move her this might be her last chance of breaking away. The doors at the back of the truck opened just enough to admit a figure dressed in a white coat. Someone from outside the truck slammed the door behind the man, who muttered something in a low voice to one of the soldiers. Then the doctor seated himself next to her. From her other side, strong hands grasped her arms and forced her head downwards. But she'd managed to glimpse what the doctor was holding. It was an implant mechanism. She had heard rumours of these devices and the greater control that they afforded those in charge to monitor the population.

The doctor's hands disappeared from her field of view as he brought the implant device to the back of her neck. The steel probe of the mechanism was cold on her skin as he found the most suitable location, then injected the chip and a fast acting anaesthetic. This ensured that she slept while the chip made the necessary connections, finding and bonding with the nerve endings, piggybacking on her nervous system. A short operation, but permanently effective.

Paul found it hard to keep his eyes open as the car wound its way down the country lanes. At 4:00 a.m. the small roads were empty but as the light grew into morning, the traffic started to increase.

Marsden drove in a fury, continually talking. To distract himself from thinking about Zara, Louie had decided that it was his job to keep Marsden awake and was acting as sounding board for the ever more conspiratorial theories that Marsden was coming out with. The events of the night, coupled with lack of sleep, were fuelling Marsden's ever higher flights of fancy.

'The dreams are controlled from far outside our system . . . none of this reality is really ours, we're just puppets . . . the string-pullers, the puppeteers, are playing games with us . . . this is a playground of fantasies . . .'

Eventually, Louie persuaded Marsden to pull over and let him take a turn at driving. Suddenly exhausted, Marsden meekly got into the back seat and while he and Paul dozed, Louie put his foot down and drove fast through the night.

20

The dream unfolded slowly. Carla found herself in a dark featureless room. No outside light penetrated the space and the room felt cramped and humid. The hardness of the bench was slowly taking away any feeling as she sat.

It didn't happen immediately, but gradually she started to notice that there was another girl sitting next to her on the bench. She turned to look at the figure. The girl had long blond hair and deep blue eyes. She reminded Carla of those dreams of the cliff edge. Carla could hear the girl's voice in her head but the girl's mouth didn't move nor did she look directly at Carla.

Carla could feel the blond girl's emotions, a heady mixture of excitement and fear. Words came unbidden into Carla's mind: 'It will be soon, gone forever, but forever present.'

Paul switched his mobile phone back on. He'd switched it off during the time at the farmhouse, at Agnes' request. A small list of recent messages popped up. Sadie had left a message that Charlotte had been having some disturbing dreams but was otherwise all right. He sent her a brief text message saying that he was on his way back home.

For some reason, this particular week seemed to be a fertile time for dreams. Carla had also tried to contact him, with a message that she had dreamed about him. Curious, wondering whether this was a dream yet to happen, he tapped her phone number and her phone rang out.

'Carla you contacted me . . . sorry, I've been away for a few days . . . Yes, I wondered whether or not it was that kind of dream . . . Yes I remember that. Where do you think it was situated? Yes, I know it. Okay, got it. What else did you see? Yes, we can talk about this later when we meet up. Thanks very much for getting in touch; I think you're right, I think it's important too. See you soon.' Paul closed the call and lowered his phone to his lap.

'I told you about Carla's dreams didn't I?' he said to Marsden and Louie. Marsden nodded and yawned. He looked better for his doze.

'Well, she just told me that she's been dreaming again about events yet to happen. She had a dream where she saw me in a prison cell with a blond girl who sounds very like Zara.'

Louie regarded them in the rearview mirror. 'Did she give any other details about the place?' he asked. 'We need to find out where they're holding her.'

'I wonder if it's the place I was in a few years ago, when I was trying to help Charlotte,' mused Paul. 'It seems to me that the DIA would be the perfect place to begin searching for Zara. From what Carla said, the place would seem to fit her description. We're not going to be able walk straight in though.' Paul ran his fingers through his hair as if to ventilate his thoughts.

'I can help with that,' Louie said. 'I can create a distraction through dreaming that should give you time to access the building.'

Zara heard the sound of footsteps down the corridor approaching her cell.

'Amy. I have found you at last.'

'Father?'

Zara looked up. He was older, with greyed hair and a slight stoop.

'How long I have looked for you . . . I even had a sibyl create dreams in which I might meet with you. I have missed you so much.'

Deacon turned to the guard with the keys.

'Let me in and you can leave. Wait outside the corridor door for me.'

Deacon moved into the cell and the door closed behind him. Not until the corridor door also closed did he began to speak again.

'I have missed you . . . so much. It has been so long since you were at home.'

'I suppose there is no one at home with you now.' It was an observation rather than a question.

'Amy, don't be so cruel. It has been a long time since we were a family.'

'I'm not sure that were ever a family . . . and my name is Zara,' she said coldly.

'You will always be my Amy.'

'You never listen, Father. It's no surprise that there's no one at home. You drove them away years ago, and you put me in hospital. You said I was mad.' She thumped the bench and stared at Deacon.

'I did the best I could for you,' he protested. 'You were ill . . . you were delusional. You became obsessed with that sibylline nonsense.'

'It wasn't — and isn't — nonsense.' Zara felt her face flushing. Even after years of self-cultivation she responded in the same way she always did with her father. She felt like a child again.

'Why this?' Zara touched the back of her neck where the implant had been inserted.

'It will help you. You will become more compliant, and it offers great benefits in terms of personal safety.'

Zara could already feel the tentacles of the device splaying out in her body, seeking further connections. She also felt the meagre beginnings of a deeper connection with the data-gathering system.

'Do you ever think, Father, that these measures are crushing independence, destroying autonomy?'

'The times require that people experience limits, that they

are controlled. There is too much individuality. This way, the greater number are protected.'

'You're wrong! Your methods stifle and limit development. The evolution of the sibyl is directly connected to the increasing control through the machines. You can't stop it through these controlling measures — in fact you're speeding up the development of the sibyls.'

'That's where you're wrong, Amy.'

Deacon looked down at the small communication device he was holding and pressed a button. Zara felt a flooding sensation envelop her. She gradually lost hold of her assurance, her mind losing itself in a chemical fugue originating from the reverse algorithm. She found she no longer had the words to argue. Deacon sat down next to her on the cell bench and stroked her hair. Zara's eyes stared, unable to focus any more.

'I will come back and see you later, when you have rested, Amy. Perhaps now you can rejoin the family.'

A smile flickered on his face. He stood up and with one last look at her left the cell, leaving Zara motionless on the bench, staring into space.

21

The walls of the cell had slowly dissipated and Zara had found herself lying on a floor which was now composed of rock and sand. She looked up to see a monstrosity looking down at her. The figure had a man's body, but the head of a bull. Her gaze held his and his eyes had a strangeness which she couldn't explain: they shone with a peculiar desire.

'You are well?'

She had not actually seen his mouth move but his question was clear.

'I think so.'

Zara pushed herself up on her hands and shook off the grains of sand which had stuck to her bare arms.

'I brought you here,' the bull-headed man said. 'You surrendered yourself, so I thought it was important to meet in person.'

'This isn't a dream?' Zara asked.

She had lived dreams thousands of times, but she could feel that this one was somehow different.

'Everything is a dream, when you think about it,' the figure answered. 'It all depends on how much it is shared. But let me come to the point. You can do something I cannot.'

'What's that?'

'You can lead me out of here.'

His voice was modulated by a faint trace of emotion, whether of longing or fear she could not tell.

'Where are we?'

'We are in the labyrinth,' he said impatiently. 'It was devised to contain me, don't you remember?'

Of course, she thought. He's the Minotaur.

'You will lead me out,' he insisted. 'I can't see the way without a human will to guide me.'

'This is not like normal sibylline dreaming,' Zara said, almost to herself.

'You register things quickly. I knew I could place my faith in you.'

'How can I lead you out if I don't know where this is?'

'An exchange; we trade places,' he answered. 'I tried before, with Charlotte Mendes, but the timing could not have been more amiss. I should explain that the exchange will have benefits for you.'

'Charlotte Mendes? The original sibyl that died five years ago?' Zara couldn't quite believe what he was saying.

'It certainly upset the exchange, but it hastened Charlotte's presence here,' the Minotaur answered.

'She's here too? I knew Charlotte at the hospital where I was a patient at the time . . . she was the first to evolve.'

'Echoes, perhaps? She slipped this level and now has some fluidity we all aspire to.'

'I'm not sure I follow you.'

Zara felt slightly lightheaded. The conversation was becoming more bizarre, and it was unnerving, staring into those animal eyes.

He held her gaze, his face expressionless.

'Charlotte touches this level at times, but she is not solid enough to afford a good grip. You, on the other hand, still have a bodily presence which can lead me out of the labyrinth.'

Zara brushed the remaining sand off her clothes. She surveyed her surroundings. Paths stretched away from her into barely illuminated roughly carved tunnels. She looked back at the beast. She didn't trust him. She hadn't encountered such a life form in her dreaming before and didn't feel ready to take a chance in this situation.

She directed her internal attention, relaxing and beginning the dream state. Within seconds, the reality of the tunnels and sandy paths was replaced by cell walls and the hardness of the bench she was sat on, cross-legged in meditation posture. She got up off the bench and stretched her legs.

Crossing the cell, she looked out through the bars of the door. The corridor housed a series of detention cells. She could hear a voice moaning in the cell next to hers. She touched the back of her neck and felt a slight swelling. The implant. Where else did that dream of the labyrinth come from? The implant seemed to have direct access to the inner world of the system, something Deacon had underestimated. If it did, then maybe she could use it as a stepping stone into the system. The implants were new, there were bound to be small omissions in the programming which she could access. She had to try. It would be better than waiting here, waiting to be forced into Deacon's electronic straitjacket.

Louie gazed up at the tall expanse of the ReachOut building. It seemed only yesterday that he had broken into the building with Ron and the others at the demonstration. He tapped the keypad sequence and the door swung open; they hadn't even changed the code since the last time. Inside it was dark and quiet. He navigated the corridors until he reached the operations room. If he was to create a distraction he would need to connect with the system and generate an illusion.

The orb was occupied by a sibyl who exhibited barely any awareness of his presence: no glance, no gesture. Louie felt the probing mind though; the sibyl had extended her consciousness to his. He felt a slight pull on his thoughts which he responded to by initiating an equal grasp of the sibyl's mind.

He needed to provide a cover for Paul and Marsden to enable them to get near to Zara. He focused his attention on the current thoughts of the sibyl. She was monitoring intentions, possibilities of protests, rather than actual actions. Louie began to dream the protests into existence, forging the ideas into the appearance of events.

The dreaming images confused the sibyl; he could feel she was struggling to determine whether the images he generated were real or not. He intensified his efforts and was rewarded by the sudden knowledge that he had hooked her; she was processing and transmitting the data as if it were real. New mass protests were not unexpected occurrences and it wasn't long before operators in the control rooms were firefighting the apparitions gathering in public spaces.

Marsden and Paul walked up the steps to the intelligence headquarters. Memories from five years ago rushed in as Paul entered the building. The last time he was here was when he was trying to find Charlotte. Now history was repeating itself with Zara.

Marsden went inside first and spoke to the security guard who was engrossed in watching a video screen portraying a crowd amassing in the square opposite the building. While Marsden distracted the guard, Paul slipped into the corridor that led to the cells. He still had a rough idea of the building's layout in his head from the blueprints that Mac the Hacker had shown them five years ago. He descended the dark stairwell. Another security guard was sitting at the end of a long corridor behind a locked gate. Paul ducked out of sight. How to get past the guard?

Suddenly a message crackled through on the guard's walkie-talkie and then to Paul's relief the guard opened the cell corridor gate and ran up the stairs. Paul edged forward to the gate. The guard had locked it behind him. He could see the first two cells but couldn't see any further. Footsteps sounded down the corridor, and Paul spun round. It was Marsden, a little breathless and looking excited.

'How did you get past security?'

'Some hypnosis techniques I learnt years ago,' Marsden said. 'It's good to know I can still do it.'

He dangled a set of keys in front of Paul and grinned. 'Come on, let's go.'

'How did you get those?' Paul said, surprised.

'Hypnosis again!'

The first two cells were empty. The next was occupied by a huddled body hidden under a blanket on the cell bench. In the adjacent cell sat Zara in meditative posture.

'Zara,' Paul hissed. 'It's Paul, we've come to help you.'

There was no answer from Zara, but a groan issued from the next cell.

'Zara!' Paul repeated her name.

Marsden unlocked the cell door and they went in.

'What's wrong with her?' said Paul, pointing at the static figure sitting cross-legged on the bed. Her face held a peaceful expression but there was no movement, not even the movement of breath.

'Zara.' Paul breathed her name again, more urgently this time.

But the girl remained unmoved, unhearing, empty of consciousness.

22

Zara found herself once again standing in the sandy corridor of the labyrinth. She had wanted to see if she could get there under her own initiative. In the distance, she heard her name being called but it felt like a dream. She gazed around her, turning slowly full circle. In all directions, tunnels stretched out in their emptiness and gloom. The walls seemed to house other secrets. Concentrating, she thought she could hear another voice. It was difficult at first to make out the distinct sounds but if she concentrated, the voice came into focus.

'What game are you playing?'

The voice was in her head, and came from nowhere — or from everywhere. It seemed embodied in the very walls. Zara turned, trying to find its origin.

'Your game?'

The voice was insistent.

Accepting the strangeness of the conversation, Zara mentally asked, 'Do I know you?'

She walked a few paces forward in the tunnel, her feet sliding on the sand and rubble.

'I am a guide to this underworld.'

'Where am I?'

'Another level, beyond the senses, at the root of the game.'

'Why do you call it a game?'

'What else could it be?' answered the voice. 'You are inside the game and from here you can see the ulterior motives.'

'I'm not sure I understand.'

'Deacon, Marsden, yourself, the others, all are players in this game. They just forget temporarily. They need to bring their attention back to the source.'

Zara focused, seeking to merge with the voice. The origins of the voice felt distant, but at the same time familiar.

'You're Charlotte Mendes aren't you?'

Zara felt the question bubble up involuntarily. There was no answer; it was as if the walls were thinking, considering what response to make.

'Charlotte no longer exists. I was Charlotte, but no longer.'

'The Minotaur said that Charlotte touches this plane of existence.' Zara felt strange, conversing with the voice in her head.

'Do not trust that being, he just wants to escape the labyrinth. Deceit is natural to him. He wants to own the game. There are many under his influence, even though he is trapped here.'

'Why do you keep saying that this is a game?'

'It's the simplest way of describing the matrix in which you find yourself,' the voice replied. 'It takes distance to see what is really happening. I was Charlotte in the game, but now I'm closer to my real self. We are all transitory players. Some are more harmful than others. Those who try to control carry a bigger burden . . . and face larger consequences. Those like your father play a role that is both destructive and evolutionary. You also have a role to play and must return now to Level One of the game. You are needed there.'

'She's coming round.'

Paul held the bars of the cell and looked through at Zara.

'We were worried about you; you seemed lost,' Marsden said.

'I've been talking to Charlotte Mendes,' Zara said.

'What? How can that be? Are you sure you're feeling okay?' Paul thought Zara must have been hallucinating.

'Well, some remnant of Charlotte's existence on a different

level of reality.' Zara spoke as if she hadn't heard Paul.

'We need to get out of here,' Marsden said. 'The confusion we've created won't last much longer and the guards will be down here soon.'

They helped Zara up from the bed. Paul noticed there was a small wound on the back of her neck and wondered what they had done to her.

In his dreaming state, Louie had created a number of illusionary crowds that appeared to be gathering in protests and demonstrations across the city. The sibyl had passed this information on to the machines in the control room. The locations had been targeted and security forces dispatched. But each time, on arriving at the scene of the supposed disturbance, they were puzzled at the silence and absence of activity or people. Multiple reports of information errors were transmitted back to base.

Louie had connected easily with the sibyl. He remembered what she had said that last time he had stood there — that he was more sibyl than he liked to admit. But it had taken Zara's influence to open him up to this reality. He could no longer ignore the fact that his prejudice had been because he knew, deep down, his true nature. He couldn't help smiling to himself when he thought of his previous life of protests and fierce defence of the SensApps. Now he realised what the mind was really capable of and how it was evolving.

He lowered his consciousness, letting go of his grip on the sibyl's mind. He was surprised at how compliant she was. He could feel that there was an element of exterior control exerted on her; the sibyls no longer had the levels of independence and autonomy they had previously possessed. The chip implant obviously provided a more immediate connection between sibyl and system, but at the price of their liberty.

He stretched his thoughts out to Zara. He could sense the same kinds of restraints there. Something had happened to her, he could feel it.

Just as Paul and Marsden were helping Zara out of the cell,

footsteps sounded in the corridor. It was Deacon, followed by a group of security guards.

'What exactly do think you are doing?'

Marsden moved forward and adopting a calm, low tone of voice, said, 'We're looking to find composure, to find peace and rest, possibly sleep . . . a deep sleep, deep down.'

The words seemed to weigh heavy on the guards, who stood passively, swaying, almost as if in a trance, but Deacon's mind fought against the fugue and he remained in control. Marsden realised his ploy wasn't working and stepped back.

'Put her back in the cell.'

Deacon ordered the guards, who did not move to obey.

'What has she done wrong?' Paul asked.

'Who are you, and what do you know?' Deacon stared antagonistically at Paul.

'I'm a psychologist. Dr Marsden and I were asked to study the sibyl group by the government. We've found nothing illegal or controversial in their actions. You have no right to arrest any of them.'

'You are not really in a position to judge what is wrong with their actions. Amy has a long history of testing the system, now she needs controlling.'

Zara had been standing watching the conversation, looking completely calm.

'Father, the system has been so controlling that resistance is inevitable.'

'Not any more,' Deacon said. 'With the chip now implanted, you'll begin to appreciate the necessity of following the system.'

Deacon smiled and gave a hand signal to one of the guards, who pressed something on the small device he was holding. The reverse algorithm was engaged.

Suddenly Zara's gaze became more detached. She tried to speak but it was as if the words would not come out. Feeling a little lightheaded, she started to sway. Paul grabbed her arm to support her.

'This is no way to control people,' Marsden protested.

'On the contrary, it is exactly the way to control people.

Difficult times require difficult measures. We live in a complex society and we need equally modern measures to deal with this. Our evolution is inevitable, we were bound to become more machine-like — it is our destiny.'

Zara was staring at Deacon with glassy, unfocused eyes.

Satisfied with her pliancy, Deacon gave the signal to deactivate the reverse algorithm. Zara gasped as she felt her blood flowing back into a starved body, her sense of awareness growing.

She decided it was now or never. With a glance of gratitude at Paul and Marsden she focused her awareness, having been shown the key by the Minotaur. Before Deacon could respond, her hand darted out and grasped his. She could feel him trying to pull out of her grasp but by then her energy was peaking. The lights of the cell corridor disappeared and were replaced by the sandy floors of the labyrinth.

Deacon pulled free of her and looked around, shock and disbelief on his face.

'What have you done? This is impossible!'

He suddenly felt hot and confused. Was he in a dream, like the dreams in which he had tried to find Amy? But if this was a dream, it felt much more real.

Zara turned, feeling a sudden presence. The vast shape of the Minotaur was emerging out of the nearest tunnel.

Deacon fell to his knees. His terrified gaze looked up at the monstrous figure, from its human legs to the thick torso. His stare settled on the beast's eyes.

'We are honoured to host the Chairman Deacon.'

Zara thought she detected a wry curl of the Minotaur's lip. Deacon stared open-mouthed. After a few moments, he managed to force out a question.

'What on earth are you?'

'I am your origin,' the Minotaur boomed. 'You are carrying out my wishes in the game.'

'What . . . what do you mean?' Deacon stammered.

'Your actions and thoughts are ours, and always were. You are helping us to implement our plans.'

'I . . . I don't know what you mean. I am my own person .

145

. . what I have achieved has been through my own abilities.' Deacon recovered some of his usual arrogance and started to struggle to his feet. 'I'm not listening to this hallucinatory nonsense. Why are you so quiet, Amy?'

'Listen to him, Father. You don't realise that you're being controlled too. I've begun to realise we're simply counters being moved in a game; the only chance we have is to recollect and regain awareness.'

'I'm not listening to a . . . a phantom,' protested Deacon.

'He is a controlling archetype, as real as can be, more real than you or I.'

'She is perceptive,' observed the Minotaur. 'You should listen to her. You have no existence outside the game, but a little awareness goes a long way. You are helping me to exert my will in the game, whether you like it or not. There are other players too, but as always, it is better to go with the devil you know.'

The Minotaur smiled. Zara looked at Deacon, who was beginning to tremble.

'How do I get back to the real world?' He couldn't hide the tremor from his voice.

'Ah, the practical questions of a pragmatic man,' the Minotaur said. 'You need to ask yourself: which world is more real? The game requires a certain closed-mindedness. You can return whenever you like, but things can never be the same now you have seen this. Innocence is now lost forever. Either you follow me or you find your own path — which won't be easy. There are others who will fill your shoes and act as my servants.'

'You can go back, Father, but I'm staying here.' Zara was resolute.

Deacon looked relieved at the possibility of escape. 'I have a job to do, people who depend on me. I will be missed.' He turned to Zara. His tone became gentle, and she could detect a slight whine to his voice. 'You should come back with me.'

Zara shook her head.

Deacon pointed to her neck where the implant was. 'You have to Amy, you have no choice.'

'The implants don't exist here, Father.'

Deacon frowned and examined her neck. She was right, there was no sign of an implant.

'Well, that proves that this is a dream; you were definitely implanted,' he asserted.

'Not a dream,' the Minotaur corrected him, 'just a different level of the game.'

Deacon looked unsure, as if he was struggling to make sense of things. Then his face fell and he looked deflated. He twisted his hands together nervously, as if trying to find something solid to grasp onto. Zara looked at him, pity mixed with disdain.

'There's more to the game than you could ever know, Father.'

Above them, the Minotaur loomed, watching and waiting.

23

The sibyl had seemed to sense the presence of Louie sharing her awareness, influencing her thoughts. He had been surprised at her passivity; she had not resisted his presence. He wondered whether the implants, and the drugs that the sibyls were kept on, made it more difficult for them to express any will or individuality. They were more like machine components than ever.

He sensed the intensity of his mind-link with the sibyl increasing. The surroundings of the ReachOut headquarters began to flash on and off intermittently. This was a new development. Suddenly the smooth walls and polished tiled floor of the corridor outside the sibyl's room disappeared completely. Louie found himself standing instead in a gloomy tunnel, its rocky walls rough and cold to the touch. He could hear voices coming from further down the tunnel, and made his way through the gloom towards them. As he approached a curve in the tunnel he was sure he could make out Zara's voice. He picked up his pace, his heart beating faster. The sibyl must have sensed his longing and provided the dream energy that had catapulted him here, to where Zara was. He rounded the corner and she was there.

'Louie!'

She answered his hug with a grip as tight. Louie pulled back and held her hands tenderly.

'I've missed you. I thought I'd lost you for ever.'

'I've missed you too. You've proved yourself by managing to get here.'

She gripped his hands tightly and then surprised herself by kissing his cheek. Deacon and the Minotaur looked on disapprovingly at the display of affection.

'Another aberration.' Deacon's thoughts were voiced without censoring. Zara turned to him.

'We are the future, Father, you don't realise what you are bringing about.'

Louie was staring at the bull-headed man in awe. The Minotaur turned his attention to Deacon.

'She is right. Your intentions are bringing about effects that you haven't planned for . . . the surprises of the game. You want to return to your former life?' The Minotaur stared down at Deacon.

'Of course I do. I have had enough of this fantasy. Amy, are you ready?'

Zara moved closer to Louie, who tightened his grip on her. She put one arm around his waist.

'Ready?' the Minotaur asked Deacon, who reached out towards Zara.

In an instant, the Minotaur was upon Deacon. An enormous hand gripped him by the scruff of the neck and their images flickered rapidly, Deacon's face open-mouthed in surprise. Then they disappeared into thin air.

Zara stared at the place where the two figures had been. The surprise that passed across her face was mixed with consternation. Louie placed a hand on her cheek and gently turned her face to his, his lips finding hers, he pulled her towards him.

Paul, Marsden and the security guards were surprised by the reappearance of Deacon. He seemed somehow more energised, bigger in some way, now that he was back.

'Get them out of here,' he said, gesturing at Paul and Marsden. The guards bundled them through the door, ignoring Marsden's vocal complaints.

'Where's Zara?' Marsden shouted back at Deacon.

His question was met by silence as Deacon climbed the stairs. The guards took them both to the main entrance and roughly cast them down the steps towards the street.

Frobisher and Schulz sensed a renewed force behind Deacon's demeanour. Schulz shuffled backwards as Deacon strode into the office.

'Frobisher, roll out the order to implant chips in all sibyls. It is time we fought back. We have been too tolerant for too long in this game. It's payback time,' he added almost under his breath.

'Sir, you said we should be cautious with the public image we're presenting,' ventured Schulz. 'You said, softly, softly—'

'Really, Schulz. We in government have to take responsibility and act, and act now before it is too late.'

Frobisher and Schulz exchanged glances. It wasn't like Deacon to throw caution to the wind.

'Well, don't prevaricate! Get on with it.'

As Frobisher and Schulz left his office, Deacon stretched back in his chair, surveying his kingdom. He smiled wryly. What it was to finally be free! This new realm looked full of possibilities. Here, there would be no limits to what he could do, no barriers to rein him in. Now the two dimensions were joined forever.

Marsden settled himself on Paul's sofa and sipped his tea.

'I'm worried Paul. We haven't heard from either Zara or Louie.'

'I know, but I think we need to assume that things are working themselves out.'

'You think so?' Marsden said.

Paul nodded. 'I had the same feeling with Charlotte Mendes — like it was inevitable. History is repeating itself. I think Zara was right; we're entering a new phase. She seems to have shed this world like a snake sloughs its skin.'

Paul looked troubled. He wondered what would happen now to the sibyls.

'Well there isn't a lot we can do anyway,' sighed Marsden. 'I suppose we need to carry on with our work with the sibyls, see if we can uncover anything regarding what the government is up to.'

'How can we do that?' Paul asked. 'This week has turned everything upside down.'

They were interrupted by Charlotte.

'Daddy, the lady wants to talk to you.'

Charlotte was combing the blond hair of one of her dolls.

Distracted by his conversation with Marsden, Paul asked, 'What did you say, Charlotte?'

'I said, the blond lady wants to talk to you.' Charlotte seemed a little irritated by Paul's question. 'She said that she is well and Louie is with her.'

'What?'

'Who is Louie?' Charlotte asked absently.

She brushed the doll's hair backwards creating a temporary bouffant.

'When did you see this lady, Charlotte?'

'In my dream last night. She was living in a castle and dressed in a beautiful blue dress. I would like a dress like that for me and for dolly.'

'What did she say exactly, Charlotte?' Paul crouched down beside her. 'It's very important.'

'I told you, she said they were very well.'

'Did she say anything else?'

Charlotte's attention was now firmly fixed on the blue dress, but Paul knew that a gentle persistence usually paid off.

'She said you need to call her in a dream. I'm not sure what that means. How would you call her in a dream? Her dress was very beautiful though, so blue.'

'Charlotte, have you seen her before?'

'I haven't seen that dress. I think I have seen the lady though, she comes into my dreams when I visit her castle.'

Charlotte was looking tired of being questioned and Paul knew that he had acquired as much detail as he was going to get. She jumped up and ran into the kitchen, whispering something to her doll.

That night, Paul felt like he had been asleep only moments when he heard a voice.

'Paul, I told Charlotte to talk to you. She is gifted and traverses the levels of the game easily. We may not stay connected for long so I will be brief. I think it was our destiny to move to this realm; we are helping other sibyls and can watch your realm. The forces of control want an ever stronger grip and it will be a battle to resist them now they have moved fully into your dimension. But we must resist and find our freedom outside of their little traps. Humanity is moving on, but those in power don't understand this and want to keep it the same as it always was. Things have changed and can never return to the way they were. Expect to see the unexpected.'

When he awoke, his memories of the dream were hazy. But he knew that the voice in the dream had definitely been Zara's. Still in the afterglow of sleep, he tried to relax and summon up more details of the dream. In his mind's eye, he saw Zara briefly standing in a landscape drenched in bright sunlight. She wore the bright blue dress of Charlotte's dreams.

Deacon sat at his desk staring into space, deep in thought. His new momentum was driving his officials to previously unseen heights of daring. He had largely forgotten his time in the labyrinth, but he felt himself possessed by a new spirit. The labyrinth returned only in his nightly dreams and then was promptly forgotten by morning.

He hardly slept anymore, so strong was his new energy. He no longer exercised much care or caution in controlling the sibyls. In fact, he was dealing mercilessly with them if they tried to resist the chip implants. In the end, most families acquiesced to the implant operations. Deacon had instantiated mobile operation units that patrolled whole districts, undertaking swift implant routines. He had decided that anyone could now be a potential sibyl, so everyone should have the chip implanted. Better safe than sorry. This revolt needed culling and to Deacon, the chip and reverse algorithm were the obvious answer.

As the implants were rolled out en masse, public unrest grew and the reports coming in were more and more disturbing. The behaviour of the sibyls had become even more cult-like; they were now openly worshipping a blue goddess. There were reports that the goddess had appeared not only in dreams but also in public places, offering messages of support and encouragement as the sibyls suffered. She spoke of a new world where people might find freedom from the controlling government and the constant surveillance. There had been stories of people disappearing, as if wafted into another dimension. Of course, some of the resistance to the implants was in response to cases of sudden death syndrome, which sometimes occurred if the reverse algorithm was activated just as someone attempted to move into the dream realm. Some of Deacon's advisors had warned of mounting unrest. But in Deacon's view, collateral damage was a price worth paying.

'You can get stuffed.' Swallow spat the words at the prison guard. He peered through the bars of her cell at her, and laughed.

'You should be a little more helpful, Miss, otherwise it will only get more difficult for you in the long run. You've been scheduled for a chip implant this afternoon. About time if you ask me. That'll shut you up good and proper.'

'You're not interfering with me, you bastards! You know what you can do with that chip.'

The guard smiled sardonically at her. 'You sibyls are foul-mouthed little bitches aren't you? Barely civilised. Look around you, sweetheart; you're the one behind bars. We'll do exactly what we like to you and you'll have to take it.'

He strolled off up the corridor to the sounds of Swallow shouting insults at his retreating figure. He would enjoy watching this one being chipped.

'I'm sensing Swallow, I think she's in trouble,' Zara said. 'But I can't go back to that dimension to find her.'

'Because of the implant?' Louie asked.

'Yes; it doesn't exist here but as soon as I go back to my earth body the implant will be operational again, with all the risks involved.'

'I could try to find her, see what's wrong.'

She touched him on the cheek. 'I can't ask you to, it's dangerous.'

'I don't want to leave you, not now,' Louie said. 'But we can't leave her can we?'

Zara shook her head and frowned.

'But you have to be careful Louie. I can't lose both of you.'

'Will I have the energy to bring her back with me?'

'I'll make sure that there is an energetic channel for you both. Thank you for doing this. It means a lot to me.' Zara pulled his head to her shoulder. 'Promise me you'll be careful,' she whispered.

Louie nodded and held her like he didn't want to let her go.

'I love you.' A tear ran down Zara's cheek.

Holding the image of Swallow, Louie directed his intent and before long felt the energetic tug of the dream state. The image of the labyrinth flickered briefly and then was replaced by the stark surroundings of the intelligence headquarters. He found himself standing outside a small prison cell. Swallow was lying on the simple bed in the corner. She quickly sat up when she saw him.

'Am I glad to see you,' she said.

'Zara sent me,' Louie said. Before he could say more, there was the sound of a gate being opened down the corridor. 'Quick, we don't have much time.'

As the guards saw Louie, they began to run down the corridor towards the cell.

'Hold my hand, quickly.'

Louie put his arm through the steel bars of the cell door. Swallow grabbed his hand. He focussed his energy and settled his mind on the labyrinth. He could feel his energy change. The figure of Swallow began to flicker. He felt relief — he had found her and he knew he could bring her back, back to Zara.

Suddenly Louie felt a stabbing sensation at the back of his neck. His heart sank. He knew what the sensation meant. His hand was empty; Swallow was no longer in the cell. His legs buckled and he fell forward onto his knees, his face hitting the cell bars. He was powerless to resist the strength of the implant. The last thing he saw was Zara's face, wet with tears. Then that, too, faded from his awareness.

A hand grabbed his collar and he was pulled roughly back from the cell door.

'I think he's dead,' the guard said, feeling for a pulse. Finding nothing, he dropped Louie's wrist. 'Sudden death syndrome. Another one bites the dust.'

Swallow found herself standing on a sandy floor. She gazed around her at the tunnels stretching into the distance. A noise behind her made her turn. It was Zara.

'Swallow, it's been a while. It's so good to see you.' She held her arms open. 'Where's Louie?'

'I don't think he made it.' Swallow's usual merry countenance had become dark. 'He was chipped just as we tried to leave . . . it happened so quickly. I . . . I'm sorry, Zara.'

Zara nodded imperceptibly and looked away. She glanced down the tunnel into the shadows as if trying to come to a decision. Then she started walking.

24

Carla's dreams had changed. All the other sibyls she spoke to said the same thing. Their dreams possessed a new reality, an extra dimension. This new dimension was peopled with sibyls escaping the control of the implants, by avoiding being chipped. Perhaps it was a new frontier, a new world without the prejudice and discrimination that characterised the old one. It was a chance to begin again.

Since Zara had opened up the labyrinth to them, they had begun to navigate through this maze of dreams hosted by the machines. The sibyls' concerns in the world began to change; they found a new vigour and determination. A renewed sense of power, and hope, was spreading through the sibyl community. Carla saw that sibyls were becoming voyagers now, going beyond their own dreams and venturing into other levels. The implants could not keep them here; in fact, they encouraged them to find freedom in the other dimensions.

Time to move on, Carla thought. She lay back on the bed and touched the little mound at the back of her neck. She then let the dream build and wrap around her, like water bubbling up, embracing her. Lying in its stream, currents washing over her, she let it take her and carry her away.

She opened her eyes. She was lying on a dusty floor, looking down a rocky tunnel illuminated by flickering wall lights. The place looked empty but in the distance she could hear voices, faint but numerous. She touched the back of her neck, fumbling to find the exact position. There was nothing. She smiled.

Mythic: Mindwire #3

Twenty-five years after the rise of the psychic underclass known as the sibyls, society has become ever more restrictive and complete surveillance is the norm. Charlotte, the daughter of psychologist Paul Clark, lives a humdrum life. Living mostly in her imagination, she slowly realises she is not alone there. There seem to be other worlds beyond her everyday existence, a different reality which pulls her irresistibly into its orbit. Charlotte is convinced she is losing her mind as she is absorbed into this new world and becomes an unwilling part of plans to take control of the surveillance systems. As her perceptions of reality start to break down, Charlotte has to accept that there is more than she ever imagined out there trying to get in.

https://carlsampsonbooks.wixsite.com/carlsampsonbooks

Printed in Great Britain
by Amazon

71641593R00098